THE HESSIAN DRUMMER
BOY OF NEWPORT

THE HESSIAN DRUMMER
BOY OF NEWPORT

Walter K. Schroder

HERITAGE BOOKS
2011

HERITAGE BOOKS

AN IMPRINT OF HERITAGE BOOKS, INC.

Books, CDs, and more—Worldwide

For our listing of thousands of titles see our website
at
www.HeritageBooks.com

Published 2011 by
HERITAGE BOOKS, INC.
Publishing Division
100 Railroad Ave. #104
Westminster, Maryland 21157

Other Heritage Books by the author:
Stars and Swastikas: The Boy Who Wore Two Uniforms: Expanded Edition
The Hessian Occupation of Newport and Rhode Island, 1776–1779

Cover illustration of a young Hessian drummer
by Joyce Halliday Smith

International Standard Book Numbers
Paperbound: 978-0-7884-5275-8
Clothbound: 978-0-7884-8599-2

*This book is dedicated
to the boys of all nations,
who were exposed to war
at an early age
because of life's circumstances.*

*This book is also dedicated
to
Emmy Hope Fox
from her
"Opa"*

CONTENTS

PREFACE   XI

CHAPTER 1   1
MY STORY

CHAPTER 2   5
THE FAMILY

CHAPTER 3   9
OUR VILLAGE

CHAPTER 4   13
ON THE FARM

CHAPTER 5   19
GOOD TIMES

CHAPTER 6   25
MARBURG

CHAPTER 7   37
MOBILIZATION

CHAPTER 8   43
THE LONG HIKE

CHAPTER 9   55
EMBARKATION

CHAPTER 10   65
"SHIPS AHOY!"

CHAPTER 11   83
OFF TO AMERICA

CHAPTER 12   93
THE HIGH SEA

CHAPTER 13   99
POINT OF NO RETURN

CHAPTER 14   107
AMERICA!

CHAPTER 15   119
NEWPORT AND RHODE ISLAND

CHAPTER 16   141
IN AND ABOUT NEWPORT

CHAPTER 17   151
    THE BATTLE OF RHODE ISLAND

CHAPTER 18   165
    SETBACKS

CHAPTER 19   177
    A NEW BEGINNING

ABOUT THE AUTHOR   181

LOCAL
AUTHOR

BESTSELLER

ISBN

PUBLISHER

Wakefield
BOOKS

Staff/Customer Recommendation

TITLE

AUTHOR

COMMENTS

RECOMMENDED BY _____ ☐ STAFF ☐ CUSTOMER

Preface

This is the story of Peter, a fictional character, who experiences life in the historical settings of the American Revolutionary War. Although his encounters are those of a drummer boy of the Hessian Ditfurth Regiment, his actions and reactions are much like those of any other youngster from anywhere around the world at the tender age of 10. In this case, one of his main concerns is to acquire a uniform quickly so he can plan on beating the drum now rather than later. He is impatient, but well mannered and caring. He looks up to his father, a Hessian Sergeant, with respect and admiration, and loves his mother, who accompanies him on their epic crossing of the Atlantic in 1776, when his father's unit is called up by their prince, the Landgrave of the Principality of Hesse, to serve the King of Britain in the colonies of North America.

Despite freezing weather, he adapts quickly to living in a flimsy tent at the time of their midwinter landing in Newport, on Rhode Island, but soon welcomes the comforts of the sturdy shelters on Thames Street, even though the furnishings have been removed by the owners prior to the arrival of the British and Hessian occupiers. Besides the uniform that his mother, a seamstress and teacher, agrees to make for him, he worries about replacing his drum, which was destroyed in a mishap during his earlier march to the sea, and the waiting ships that would take him and his family across the ocean to North America.

Even at his very young age he is hailed as a highly dependable and sought-after drummer among King George III's 6,000 troops in Newport. He is so well liked that he is chosen to accompany the advance guard of Hessian Chasseurs during their pursuit of the retreating enemy in August of 1778. During their subsequent encounter with Continental and Black troops at what became known as the Battle of Rhode Island, Peter suffers the ill fate of being captured and losing his second drum. Luckily, his imprisonment at the Butts Hill Fort lasts but a short time, after which he hikes back to Newport alone and is stopped en route by various patrols in the countryside who question how it is that this lone Hessian boy made it to the Butts Hill area before the area had been recaptured.

Grief strikes when he learns that his father, his hero, lost his life advancing on the enemy in the open area below Butts Hill.

After departing Newport in 1779, the Hessian and British troops are reassigned to areas further south on America's east coast; this followed by their surrender at Yorktown. And in 1783, when hostilities have completely ceased, Peter is returned to Europe to await his discharge from service.

Happy to have returned a survivor, Peter is quite disappointed to learn that his widowed mother had married his father's older brother and that their newborn son would eventually inherit the family farm. Almost 18 now, Peter has to decide between working for his uncle as a farmhand, or to seek employment elsewhere. His inner most feelings determine his choice.

ACKNOWLEDGMENTS

The Hessian Drummer Boy of Newport is based on my earlier nonfiction title: "The Hessian Occupation of Newport and Rhode Island, 1776-1779." The fictional elements of the present narrative were adapted from my personal experiences as a "boy soldier" during a time when survival took on a greater meaning than victory or defeat.

I wish to thank Joyce Halliday Smith (JHS), artist and illustrator, for designing the cover painting of a young Hessian drummer, and for developing a series of spot illustrations highlighting key features of the narrative.

A special word of thanks to Anthony Orzech, artist, for granting permission to use his illustration of a Hessian gauntlet, which previously appeared in the publication: "The Hessians; Journal of the Johannes Schwalm Historical Association," Vol. 10, 2007.

Other sources of illustrations are hereby acknowledged with sincere appreciation: Revolutionary Defences of Rhode Island, by Edward Fields, 1896; Hessisches Militär, 1672-1806, by Uwe Böhm, Germany, 1986; Pierre Ozanne, at Library of Congress; Harvard University; Hessisches Staatsarchiv, Germany; and illustrations by Lora (LCS) and Walter (WKS) Schroder.

I extend a special word of thanks to Mary Schachtel Wright, middle school teacher, and to BG. Richard Valente, USA, (retired), for reading the raw manuscript and providing valued comments and suggestions.

I also thank the following for giving of their time to provide formal review comments on the completed work:

Matthew L. Blaser, chairman of the Department of English at North Kingstown High School; Sue Maden, a historical researcher and writer; and Jeffrey McDonough, publisher of the Jamestown Press.

I thank the Jamestown Press, in particular, the previously mentioned Publisher Jeffrey McDonough, and also Dara Chadwick, editor, and Melissa Wicks, production manager, for their great job of shaping my rough manuscript into a well formatted and attractive piece of work in which I take great pride and satisfaction.

Last, but not least, I thank my dear wife, Lora, for encouraging me to pursue this, my latest writing endeavor, and for providing many worthy comments during the development of the manuscript.

Walter K. Schroder

North Kingstown, R.I.

CHAPTER 1

My Story

My name is Peter Bauer. I became a Hessian drummer boy in 1776, when I was 10 years old. Since then, I have been assigned to the Ditfurth Regiment, where my father had been a Sergeant until he was killed in 1778. He died a few miles north of the town of Newport, during a battle fought on Rhode Island, then a British colony in North America. Our Landgrave, Prince Friedrich II of Hesse-Kassel, had agreed to make some 12,500 soldiers available under contract to the King of England to help him put down a serious rebellion of the colonists in America. The colonists had refused to pay taxes levied upon them by their sovereign, King George III. They also committed other traitorous acts that included civil disobedience, which culminated in an open revolution.

I was away from our village in the Hessian principality for eight years. I am fortunate to be returning home with the remnants of our regiment. I am waiting to be mustered out when I turn 18. From now on, life will be different. All I really know how to do well is beat the drum, often while the enemy is shooting at me at close range. I do have knowledge and experience in military life and procedures, from formal drills into field formations. However, such specialized skills will have limited application in our peaceful rural community, unless there is a chance of becoming a gendarme, or perhaps a Jäger – a forest ranger.

If things don't work out, I can always apply to the Landgrave to enlist me in one of his regiments as a regular soldier, based on my prior service in the British colonies in North America. I hope that my father's long and faithful service to the Landgrave, or prince as some call him, would be weighed favorably. I'll just have to wait and see if my Uncle Franz, who has been working the family farm while we were away, has need for a hand with some extra muscle to boot.

When I think about it, agricultural work might be an option for me. I performed all kinds of chores on the family farm before we left for the American colonies in 1776. That was when Grandfather Bauer was still alive. What I learned would come in handy if Uncle Franz hired me now that I am a few years older and a bit stronger. I am certainly eager to learn and work hard to help support our family.

Tending cows and feeding and grooming the horses had been a part of my daily routine some years ago. Raking hay and harvesting the various fields of grain and potatoes are also things I have done, starting when I was only six years old. Of course, I didn't handle any heavy bags or baskets, but I sure could do that now. As I think positively of what I have to offer despite my young years, I am encouraged, and I look to a successful and productive life after I shed my uniform and identity as being the Ditfurth Regiment's Drummer Boy.

Yet, as I think back on the time I spent with the regiment, I find many positive facets of that earlier life that encourage me to seek a military career, just as my father did. Regrettably, the circumstances under which he ultimately served and carried out his duties in the end did not permit him to finish his career as he had hoped he might. Now that I again stand safely on Hessian soil, I am forever thinking of my association with the soldiers of the Landgrave's army. I also think about my dear mother, who accompanied us on the long journey and voyage across the ocean, and how she always helped when help was needed. The sacrifices made by her and all others with whom I came in contact left long-lasting and positive impressions upon me as to the good of humankind. Thus, my thoughts to this day often concern themselves with things of the past, and the people I have met or known, even from among the colonists. The situations I witnessed and the experiences I enjoyed, as well as those that were less than pleasant, have contributed to my growing up and maturing. I often recall the days of my childhood, the life in our modest home and the times I worked on the farm, happy and free as a bird. But even

then, I looked up to my Father, admiring him in his smart uniform, wishing I too could become a soldier. Much has changed
over the past eight years; things are no longer as they were when
we sailed to North America in 1776, with the Hessian army hired
by Britain's King George III. Now I ask: What will my future be?
Only time will tell. Only God knows.

CHAPTER 2

The Family

When I was born in the fall of 1766, the River Lahn near our village had gone over its banks, so I was told, flooding nearby fields where my grandfather, Opa Bauer, had been working most of his life. Some of his crops along the river's edge were lost to the swiftly moving waters. The sudden and heavy three-day downpour was sufficient to destroy much of the work his family had put into the fields, hoping for another year's harvest. They say Opa Bauer was saddened and furious at the same time, but he had experienced unwanted flooding before. It didn't take him long to sit down and talk with his two sons, Uncle Franz the older of the two, and my father, Karl, to make plans for the days ahead, when the water subsided. He depended heavily on my father's ability to get a leave of absence from his regiment to help on the farm in this time of need. My mother tells me that my arrival at that time was a sign that everything must start anew. So I was off to a normal beginning, despite the chaos caused by the overflowing Lahn River.

As was customary, Franz, the oldest son, would one day inherit the farm when Opa Bauer was no longer able to handle the many chores and care for the animals. Knowing his predestined future, Uncle Franz began working the farm alongside his father, starting at an early age.

Since he was the younger of the two sons, my father had to seek other means to support a family. He had married my mother, Anna, in 1764 when they were both 19. Mother was a seamstress. Despite her age, she was already a whiz at sewing and became known throughout the village for the quality of her work. She had been a very smart student when growing up and she knew how to read and write as well as the people who taught her. Arithmetic became her favorite subject. Whenever there were things to figure out and calculate, she was always the fastest to come up with correct answers. Because of this, she developed an avocation to pass on her knowledge and teach. I was probably her first student. She taught me to count and write as soon as I was able to understand the subjects to her satisfaction. That early learning placed me in a favored position when I first joined the parson's classes. It made it easy for me to keep up with his more organized and rigorous teaching methods. My mother also encouraged me to use the old slate board that she still had from her own childhood days. I liked it, but using the hard and scratchy slate pencil to write and draw gave me goose bumps.

In those days, my papa worked at the family farm whenever he could, especially during the spring planting season, and again at harvest time. Whenever possible, he worked at one of the prince's estates not far from home, grooming and training horses. One day, when I was a few years older, he showed off his favorite mare called Mamatschi. The horse was beautiful, a real show stopper. Papa told me it was the Landgrave's favorite and had to be well groomed at all times, in case the prince suddenly called for her. Papa was overjoyed when he could ride and exercise this special horse around the estate. He often sang to Mamatschi when he was out of range of others' hearing.

A year before I was born, my father enlisted in the Landgrave's Ditfurth Regiment. He received his initial training at a site just outside Marburg, on the river Lahn, a few miles from the castle of Landgrave Friedrich II of Hesse. This worked out nicely; he was stationed close to our village, which allowed him to get home for an overnight stay every now and then after completing his recruit training. Becoming a soldier was a new way of life for him. He hailed from a farmer's family, where he had learned how to work the land. As a soldier, he learned to defend the land should need arise and the Landgrave require his troops to take to the field. After dousing his work clothes, he was outfitted with a complete wardrobe of military clothing, consisting of a Prussian blue jacket, white leggings and vest, black gaiters, shoes, socks and a field hat.

He was also issued an assort-
ment of accouterments that
included black and white
belts, a sword, a musket, a
bread bag and gear to hold
and carry musket balls and
gunpowder. They even pro-
vided all recruits with a set
of personal underwear.
My papa was quite a
sight when he came home
wearing his colorful uni-
form. It really stood out, and
his appearance was impressive. He looked so tall wearing a high field cap, itself
more than a foot in height.
His uniform sleeves were
tailored short, so they
wouldn't get in his way while
at the same time giving him
the appearance of being
even taller than he really
was. I remember him telling
me that the skimpy clothes
were issued intentionally, so
the Landgrave's soldiers
would appear extra tall in
the face of an enemy. In fact,

the Landgrave had followed the example of his powerful ally,
Frederick the Great of Prussia, who had dubbed his own soldiers:
"The tall fellows."

What surprised me even more was that my father no longer
walked with the relaxed gait we were accustomed to seeing. Since
becoming a soldier, he stood tall at all times, no longer slouching.
When walking, his steps always seemed to be following the
cadence of some distant drum beat. He had become a true soldier
in heart and soul. But that did not preclude him from taking me
fishing in the Lahn River when he had time off from soldiering.

Whenever we were lucky enough to hook carp and pike, we proudly carried our catch home so mother could cook up a nice fish dinner.

Because of his love for horses, Papa came home on horseback whenever he was granted permission to do so, which allowed him to travel faster than on foot. That gave him more time to spend with us. I was always inquisitive about his life and duties, forever querying him about what it was like being a soldier. He must have guessed that I was beginning to formulate thoughts and ideas about my future.

CHAPTER 3

Our Village

My ancestors had settled along the banks of the Lahn
River even before Grandpa Bauer was born. That was
long ago. Since that time, our family made the area their home.
Over a period of several generations, the Bauers developed into a
farming family, homesteading on the edges of a small settlement
named Kirchdorf about 200 years ago. The village is situated
across the Lahn River, about eight kilometers south of the town of
Marburg. It is a beautiful spot. Individual homes and farms line
the narrow country road that generally runs in a southwesterly
direction, making it a narrow settlement about two kilometers
long. No matter which direction one might look, the scenery is
exceptionally attractive. Not too far away to the north, we can see
the Landgrave's castle towering majestically over Marburg from a
hill high above the river. On the side of the village facing the river,
the view across the fields of wheat and rye gives the appearance of
waves in a lake whenever there is a brisk breeze. On the eastern
side of the village, the fields and crops extend almost as far as the
eye can see into the hilly countryside, and beyond into darker
areas of dense forests. Here and there, one can observe rows of
cultivated trees, giving the appearance of apple orchards or a
similarly laid out planting of other fruit trees. While most of the
fields were planted for harvesting, there were sections set aside as
pastures, reserved for feeding local cattle. Hay was harvested from
idle sections of land and stored in the barns as winter feed. Just
observing the cows at rest in the meadows spattered with wild
flowers provides a feeling of peace and tranquility, a feeling that

our world is precious, a special place to behold and enjoy.

Farms and private homes abut Kirchdorf's main street, with the working fields of the farms extending outward away from the settlement. Among the properties scattered inside the village is a general store that carries most of the essentials required by the townsfolk, such as farm-grown food items and a variety of staples brought in from nearby towns and villages. A bakery supplies all the bread the villagers could ever want. The village also has a butcher skilled in slaughtering cattle for meat and making sausages, and a dairy that provides milk, cheeses and related items to round out the diets to which the people are accustomed.

The two churches in Kirchdorf are in the village, but on different sides of the street, about a half-mile from each other. Our family attended the evangelical church each Sunday, except during harvesting time when, according to Opa Bauer, the farm work took priority over anything else. Our church became known for its superb choir. Their voices were like those of angels – touching and inspiring.

Our parson also taught school three days a week, using the small assembly area in the church as a classroom. He had been a teacher before he became our minister. Most of the time, he would have from five to 10 students of various ages in attendance. Being taught at home by my mother allowed me to keep up with the other children, especially when I'd frequently miss classes when helping out at the farm.

A small, but beautiful Catholic church down the street from ours was attended by some of the family's close friends and neighbors. Their organ could be heard every Sunday, especially when they had the windows open. This attracted some of the townsfolk, who wandered down the street to hear better and enjoy the majestic music. We only had a piano at the evangelical church, which was sufficient for our choir's needs, but still, I always wished we, too, would someday have an organ of our own. I remember one time, when the Catholics invited our choir to sing with them during a church festival. Their organ and choir, combined with the voices of our famous choir, kept the townspeople in awe, a sign that together, we could make things happen.

In a way, our village was, and still is, self sustaining. For the most part, the people work on the farms – the farmers grow fruits, vegetables and raise cattle. A windmill on a nearby hill produces flour for baking from the grain supplied by the farmers. Finally, the folks frequent the local stores to acquire needed foodstuffs with the wages the families earn for working the farms. Then, there are the various tradesmen who offer services to the people and to the farmers, such as a blacksmith, a boot maker, carpenters, chimney sweeps, a doctor and midwife, a veterinarian, a tailor and even a seamstress like my mother, who makes the clothes for our family and for others who may ask.

While the majority of the workers look forward to being paid for their labors in hard currency, some are willing to barter, particularly if it is favorable to their needs. Sometimes, farmers would be short on cash and offered eggs, bacon, potatoes and other essential items in place of standard currency as payment for their work.

CHAPTER 4

On the Farm

About 30 farming families lived in our village. In his day, my Opa's father was given an opportunity to acquire land from the Landgrave, who at that time was the landlord over all fields and property in his principality. They constructed a deal for the Bauer family to be granted ownership of the buildings and land of the farm they were working, in return for maintaining the property and providing a set percentage of their produce to the Landgrave each year.

My Opa told me some years later that the arrangement had worked out to everyone's satisfaction. The other farmers of Kirchdorf entered into similar agreements.

The farms are adequately spaced away from each other, with

15 or so on each side of the road running through town.
Interspersed among them are other people's homes, stores and
businesses, and the churches. Several farms are set back from the
road a short distance, with a path leading to them. A common
area or marketplace is located about halfway through the village.

Essentially, the farm buildings are laid out to form a square,
with gates on two ends and a farmyard between. Each has a portal
facing the village street, with doors large enough for wagons
loaded with hay to pass through to the interior of the yard without
difficulty. At our farm, the building closest to the street is our

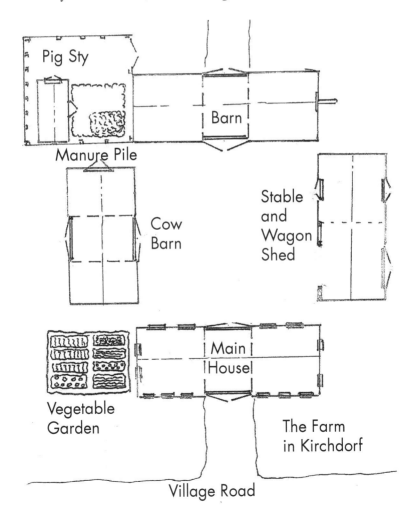

home, with the bedrooms on the second floor. The main building is large enough to accommodate the entire family. Opa had lost his wife before I was born. That left him alone with Uncle Franz, who never married and spent most of his time with him at the farm. Our small family also had living spaces that were sufficient for our needs. When Papa enlisted in one of the Landgrave's regiments, some additional space in our modest quarters was freed up.

Connected at an angle on the right end of the main house, a barn was used as a shed for Opa's wagons, and as stables for his four horses. The building directly across the yard housed 20 cows and fodder. Across the yard, opposite the main house, a two-story barn with big doors provided access to the fields and beyond. Potatoes and turnips were kept in the cellar area until sold to the market in town and in nearby settlements. The grain was kept in large storage bins above ground until it was taken to the windmill, where it was turned into flour, which was then taken to the bakery. The upper level was the hayloft where I always liked to play and hide when I was able to climb the steep ladder to get up there. On the side of the barn nearest the corner to the pigsty was a pit where the manure from the cows and the pigs was collected until it was time to spread it on the fields and plowed under. Opa told me we could thank the cattle and their manure for the fertile soil that produced the great crops the family enjoyed each year. The one element he could not control, of course, was the weather. While it could get very hot and dry at times, especially in mid summer, we could pretty much depend on rain in the amounts needed for the plantings in our fields to survive the occasional dry spell.

From the time I was six years old, I was given some minor chores around the farm that I could handle and that would instill in me a sense of responsibility and belonging. For instance, mother called on me to pick weeds in the vegetable garden she had laid out on the side of the main house, and to keep the plants watered. After mealtimes, she had me dispose of the scraps and leftovers at the manure pile and on the way back, bring a quart of milk to the house that Opa or Uncle Franz would hand me at the cow barn. Oh yes, I did trip one day and drop the enameled milk jug, spilling the fresh warm milk in the yard. Mother knew I had not been paying attention and had been daydreaming along the way, but she didn't scold me. Her words: "Let's not waste the milk like that any more," were sufficient for me to stay alert and focused while I was doing the chores. I was also recruited almost daily to take a broom much bigger than myself to sweep a barn floor or some other area that needed tidying up. It was always a clumsy operation to manage that big broom, and it took me a long time to sweep an area to their liking.

As time went on and I got a little older, my responsibilities around the farm increased proportionately. Eventually, I helped with the spring planting of rye, wheat, oats and even potatoes. Then, came the harvesting of hay. I was a few years older by then and I could turn the hay with a two-pronged pitchfork to help it dry faster. Later in the year when Opa cut the grain crops with his scythe, I followed with Uncle Franz and tied sheaves so they could be set up for drying. When that job was finished, my mother and I went out to comb the fields once more to pick up anything that had been missed.

The potato harvest was too big a job for me as a youngster. Hired townsfolk followed Opa or Uncle Franz as they operated the horse-drawn potato digger-slinger that dug deep into the soil and

scattered the potatoes about. The grown-ups were forever hustling to fill their large baskets and dump them into a waiting wagon. At the same time, they were trying to keep up with the machine that would return to unearth another row of potatoes. For the farmer, there was no stopping; the workers had to keep up with his pace.

Once the potatoes were brought in, Uncle Franz would take me along when he went back to plow the field. At that time, I would follow him with a smaller basket and pick up any stray potatoes he might kick up during that operation. Later, manure would be spread about and plowed under the field. The soil would then be given a season's rest before the next planting that might consist of oats or barley, depending on the schedule of land use Opa had developed for his farm and to which he adhered to religiously.

The one job I liked most when I was about eight or nine years old was to tend the cows in the meadow near the river's edge at the far end of the property. I did this mostly during the summer, when there was little else for me to do on the farm. In the morning, we would let the cattle out of the barn and head them along the path that leads to the river. The cows surprisingly knew their way. They just kept walking along the narrow path without venturing into the fields to their left or right. Uncle Franz's dog, Hasso, stayed near me, always ready to redirect any cow that wandered off. Once in the meadow, I laid in the grass and gazed into the sky, enjoying life and the countryside, while Hasso patrolled the perimeter of the small herd. Most of the time, all went well.

Around noon, Mother, or perhaps one of the maids Opa had hired, would bring lunch to me in a basket with a nice cup of coffee, which I thoroughly enjoyed. They included coffee, which I would otherwise not be allowed to partake of because it was a no-no for children. But, having to stay in the meadow all day long guarding Opa's herd of cattle elevated me to some higher level, perhaps into the category of grown-ups, and their entitlement to a good cup of coffee. I would carry the basket home with me in the evening when Hasso and I headed the herd back to the farm.

I thought so then, and still feel the same today: The days of my childhood, including working on the farm, will always be among the most memorable and enjoyable times of my life.

CHAPTER 5

Good Times

About the time I was nine, in the fall of 1775, Papa came home for a few days, this time riding the Landgrave's most favorite horse, Mamatschi. Of course, he was thrilled to no end at being allowed to ride Mamatschi all the way to Kirchdorf. Both my mother and I were happy for our soldier, who just kept on smiling as we stared at him in wonderment, trying to figure out how he had managed to weasel his way into being permitted to take the Landgrave's special horse out of Marburg and his nearby estate. While father stashed the saddle and bridle, we kept talking about his journey home. It wasn't far, but he did have to ride along the Lahn River, passing the places where we had gone fishing from time to time. He, too, reminisced about those days, and didn't forget to mention that I had been all thumbs at first when it was time to put a worm on a hook. I recalled it had taken some teaching on his part before I felt at ease enough to do it myself.

After he put up Mamatschi in an empty stable for the night, making sure the mare had been fed and brushed, he came into the house for supper. Mother had cooked up one of his favorite meals: a pork roast with gravy, potato balls, and red cabbage. That went to his heart and we could tell he loved every bite. What a surprise it was, for me especially, when mother brought out a freshly baked streusel cake, and then placed a cup of hot coffee in front of each of us. I gave my father a sly look, not knowing what he might say. There was no reaction on his part, so I looked at mother. She just smiled. 'What's going on?' I thought. It wasn't until later that I realized this was actually a celebration: Papa had been promoted to sergeant in the Ditfurth Regiment, and as an additional reward, the Landgrave, knowing how much he loved Mamatschi, made the day special by granting him permission to take the horse home for the weekend so he could show it off. Father had told the Landgrave how much he had spoken about Mamatschi to his friends in Kirchdorf during the time he had worked at the

Landgrave's estate before becoming a soldier. My family appreciated the Landgrave and realized that he did have feelings for his people and subordinates despite his high rank and station in life, and re-thought their earlier assessment of him as being some-what aloof when dealing with his subjects.

It was just before bed-time when Papa, knowing how interested I was in mil-itary life, asked if I would like to travel to Marburg one day so he could show me around to see for myself how soldiers live, and what they do. This was the greatest thing my father could have asked. "Yes, yes!" I said. I wanted very much to go to the castle in Marburg and see all the soldiers. He told me that having been recently promoted made it easier for him to arrange for my visit in the company of my mother. Oh, I would have to be escorted, I thought. On inquiry, he let me know that children visit-ing the castle could do so only on official invitation and in the company of an elder. And, only grown-ups and parents were ever favored with an invitation from the Landgrave. It made a lot of sense the way he explained it to me. I went to bed all excited. I kept thinking of the trip, the castle, the soldiers and of maybe even seeing Landgrave Friedrich II of Hesse-Kassel. I didn't get much sleep that night and I was still all fired up the following morning.

After a hearty breakfast of dark rye bread, butter, liverwurst and jam, Papa asked if I wanted to go fishing down the river, near the cow pasture. When I showed him how much I would like to go, he turned to my mother and said, "Anna, pack a basket for the three of us. Let's all go fishing today. It's our time to celebrate and have fun together." It turned out to be a most memorable day. Hasso tagged along, perhaps under the impression that the cows would be there too, because we took the path the herd usually followed. We only caught two small fish. When the catching didn't get any better, Papa and I jumped in the river for a swim while mother set up an abundant picnic lunch on a tablecloth she placed on the ground. It was one of a few beautiful table covers she had stitched herself and decorated with some neat flower patterns, making it a special setting fit for our new sergeant and his family. We talked and laughed until the sun started to go down and it was time to head back to the farm. Mamatschi had been fed in the morning and put in a fenced pasture for some exercise. Now my father wanted to take the mare for a run before dark. This meant getting back quickly without dilly-dallying. This was when Papa's military spirit showed. Before long, the three of us were heading up the trail in a marching step. That too, was great fun. Mother kept saying, "Slow down, slow down," but she kept up with the two of us.

The next day, when we had completed dinner and were sitting around chatting, Papa said, "I have something I'd like to share with the two of you, but you are not to speak of this to anyone, not even Opa or Franz. You understand?" Both Mother and I responded in the affirmative, as he continued: "Word is out that King George III of England will be sending an emissary to meet with our Landgrave in the very near future, presumably to inquire if Hesse-Kassel could make available a large contingent of soldiers to reinforce the King's men in his North American colonies. We were told the American colonists have become rebellious and are refusing to pay the taxes levied upon them by the King. A show of strength on behalf of their sovereign should serve well to calm their tempers. To do this, King George III may be asking for 12,000 or so Hessian soldiers and officers to serve alongside British troops in North America for a period of a year or two. An arrangement to make some of the Landgrave's regiments available for that purpose could prove highly beneficial. Both the Landgrave and the principality of Hesse-Kassel could benefit very nicely. It was envisioned that we would remain under command of our present superiors, and that the King would be reimbursing the Landgrave for our services at whatever deal they may negotiate. The money collected by the Landgrave would cover our services and any other expenses that may be incurred as a result of such an overseas expedition. The Landgrave is known to be very sharp when it comes to finances. He will undoubtedly also make sure that the families of the Hessian expeditionary force will be well taken care of."

Mother commented: "Anything like this can be very far-reaching and could affect some of the families adversely in the event of a delay or curtailment in the receipt of their soldiers' contribution to the family budget. What will the Landgrave do to protect our farms and land if he agrees to hire out most of his troops? All of this seems a bit scary to me. It seems we'd be better off if we could go along to support our soldiers one way or the other, but I imagine that won't even be mentioned."

I was all ears. Wow! How exciting.

Papa answered Mother by saying: "I am sure arrangements will be made that family support will continue without interruption. As far as protecting Hesse-Kassel while the large expeditionary force is overseas, you must realize that the Landgrave actually has an army of at least 16,000 men, and even more. And, a few years back, the Prince put into place some very thorough and effective recruiting and drafting regulations that could be implemented momentarily, if needed. What I see will happen is, there will be an accelerated recruiting effort, combined with a draft of non essential citizen-workers that could be enlisted rather quickly to fill the ranks of those serving overseas. Regarding the possibility of some of the families joining their soldiers on the expedition to America, there actually has been some chitchat about that, too. While nothing is official about anything we are talking about, there does seem a possibility that some of the non commissioned officers, that is, sergeants like myself, could be given an option to bring some family members along if there is a good chance they can be of service to their respective regiments. In our case, I think we'd be all set. Anna, I would imagine you'd be willing to provide troop support as a seamstress and tailor, and if needs arise to function as a nurse's assistant? If things remain peaceful and quiet, you might even think of giving the cooks a hand. What do you think?"

She replied in the affirmative and seemed content with Papa's explanations.

"As for you, young Master Peter," my father continued, "I think we could find a spot for you too, where you could be productive despite your young age. Perhaps a tambour, a regimental drummer boy . . ."

I jumped up, "Papa, do you mean it, could I be a drummer boy? Oh please, Papa, make it come true."

"Well," he said, "there are many things still unanswered. First, we have to wait and see how serious King George III is, and what he is willing to offer the Landgrave. It all depends on the contract terms they may agree to, and most certainly, that Friedrich II of Hesse feels he is coming out ahead. After all, to him it's a business deal, but one involving the lives of many of his loyal followers. So, any offers made by the King must be evaluated in light of the possible consequences of their acceptance. An expedition to North America to demonstrate and show off our strength in a peaceful setting could turn the campaign, if one wanted to call it such, into a pleasant tour of duty. However, should we be required to meet force with force, even though we don't believe it will ever come to that, then we have to be prepared to accept casualties among our own ranks, something we do not wish to think or talk about at this time. Like I said, too many things remain unanswered. We don't even know if any of this will ever come to pass. Let's see what the new year brings. The latest word is that the King's emissary may be meeting with the Landgrave at the castle in Kassel sometime in mid-January, 1776. Maybe they'll decide to come to Marburg instead. Who knows? I imagine I will have more to tell you when I come home for Christmas. In the meantime, I'll try to arrange a time for you, Peter, to come visit me at Marburg before the winter weather sets in."

CHAPTER 6

Marburg

Soon after Papa returned to his unit in Marburg, he arranged for my visit to the castle, in the company of my mother, to tour the ramparts and observe members of the Landgrave's Ditfurth Regiment while on duty. When word was received a few days later, Uncle Franz agreed to make the 12-kilometer trip in one of Opa's wagons. He told us that he would drop us off near the gate to the castle, and would then pick up supplies from various merchants in town while we were visiting with his brother, Karl. We agreed that he would meet us outside the gate later that afternoon, which would allow us to return to the farm at a reasonable hour to unload the supplies before dark. Getting back the same day also gave Uncle Franz time to start harvesting a patch of potatoes the next day, as he had been planning.

By six o'clock in the morning on the day we had agreed to go, Uncle Franz had hitched up two of Opa's best horses, and while smoking a pipe, was waiting for us to join him for the 12-kilometer trip. Knowing that we would be visiting inside the castle, mother had dressed up in a full skirt and laced shoes, and was wearing a bonnet. I had shined my shoes and dressed in the clothes I usually wore to church on Sundays. As we walked out the door, we looked at each other and smiled. Uncle Franz was surprised to see us in our best getups. Nodding his approval, he said, smiling: "You look very attractive, Anna, and you, young Master Peter, look like a fine young man. You should both impress the folks at the castle. I'll be waiting to hear how you make out."

It was close to seven when we pulled out of the yard. Uncle

Franz took the main road through Kirchdorf in a northerly direction, toward Marburg. It was a nice ride, a little bumpy in the wagon, but we saw many cultivated fields with farmers working their various crops, as well as meadows with small herds of cows and sheep. In some of the orchards we passed, we saw people picking apples and other fruits. We were talking all the way and laughing at almost anything. It sure was fun.

As we drew closer to our destination, we could make out some of the details of the castle hovering over Marburg and the Lahn River below. It gave me the impression that it served like a protective umbrella for the town and its people, who knew the Landgrave was indeed their protector. A while later, we entered the town, leaving the dirt road to travel on cobblestone streets. We were among houses of post-and-beam construction. Many were two stories high; a few even had a third floor. All appeared to be well maintained. The care the inhabitants were giving to their homes was reflected in the pretty flowers most of them had planted in nicely painted window boxes. Most of the people walking about were well dressed. Others in work clothes were sweeping in front of their houses or tending their narrow gardens on the sides of some of the buildings. As we went farther into town, houses and businesses were cramped much closer together, often built against each other, which gave the appearance of having been squeezed in. This type of construction made me think how different it was living on a farm, like our family. We always had lots of room and plenty of fresh air to breathe. In town, the air was dense and smoky from the many hearths and fireplaces on both sides of the street, and the streets beyond, something hardly found in Kirchdorf. On one of the roofs, I watched a chimney sweep making his way to a smoke stack, balancing himself along the roof's edge, carrying his rope and brushes. It struck me as a dangerous job and one I wouldn't want. I pointed out the man to my mother. She told me there were many ways to make a living, and that most people do their best if given the chance to employ their given talents and abilities. Maybe this man felt confident walking along roof peaks. To him, being up there above everyone else and being able to look down on everything may have given him a feeling of superiority, of being the master of the roofs and chimneys. At the same time, he may have felt free from all the pressures that existed at street level.

I gave it some thought while we were moving along and had to agree with the things mother had said. She was smart, I said to myself. The klippity-klap of our horses continued as our wagon headed up a steep and paved incline toward Marburg. When we arrived at the gate, Uncle Franz helped my mother get off the rig, while I jumped down on my own. Uncle Franz wished us good luck as he headed back down the steep incline toward town, where he would be doing his shopping for farm supplies while we were visiting.

We walked toward the portal with the large oaken gate and the guard who had been standing at attention ever since we arrived. As we approached, he lowered his musket and asked my mother for her identification. She said, "We have come to visit Sergeant

Karl Bauer of the Ditfurth Regiment."

"Oh yes", he said. "He told me to expect you sometime this morning. You may go through the small opening in the gate. Above the first door on the right, you will see a sign 'Wachstube.' Go in there and tell them your business. They will let Sergeant Bauer know you are here."

Mother thanked the guard for his help as we headed through the portal looking for the guard house sign.

As we headed through the gate, we noticed that the walkway and road leading to the interior of the castle had been paved with large cobblestones, much larger than those used to pave the streets in town. Some grooves made by wagon wheels over many years were also noticeable, particularly those running through the portal, a sign that the castle must be very old. As the sentinel said, the first door to the right was that of the guard house. We entered the room after stepping up three high granite risers. I followed my mother as she introduced herself to one of several soldiers on duty inside. The young soldier closest to the door turned to her and asked: "Madam, can I be of any help to you?"

She replied: "Yes, we are here to visit Sergeant Bauer."

"Oh yes," said the soldier, " The sergeant mentioned earlier that you would be arriving early in the day. Wait here and I will let the orderly room know you have arrived. Why don't you relax and take a seat in the meantime."

Mother thanked the soldier as he was leaving and we sat down, watching the others in the room. There were three of them. They were wearing the same uniform my father had worn when he came home, so they, too, must be from his regiment. Shortly after, two of the soldiers stepped outside, one carrying a long musket and the other a sword. I stood up and walked to the door to watch them. In front of the guard house, they stood at attention next to each other and then stepped out heading through the portal toward the gate. A few minutes later, the soldier with the sword returned in the company of the soldier who had been the guard at the gate when we arrived. I was told later that a short 'changing of the guard' ceremony had taken place. The Corporal carrying the sword had the duty of giving orders to relieve the guard we had seen earlier because he had been at his post for four hours and his tour of duty was up. Now, he wouldn't have to stand guard again for eight hours, giving him time to eat and rest. When he entered the guard house, he noticed us sitting there.

"Hello again," he said. "I see you are still waiting."

"Actually, we haven't been here that long," Mama replied. "And one of the soldiers left not too long ago to notify the orderly room."

"It shouldn't take much longer, then," said the soldier as he sat down on a stool. He then placed his musket across his knees and began rubbing the barrel with a piece of buckskin he took from his pouch. When he finished, he placed his weapon in a rack among other muskets along the wall. He had noticed that I had been following his every move, and said: "We have to keep our piece clean and spotless at all times, so we polish whenever we get a chance. In addition, it is a requirement to clean the weapon whenever we are relieved from guard duty." It impressed me that soldiers always seemed to be busy doing something.

Just about then, Papa skipped up the stairs of the guard house, with a big smile on his face. "I am so happy to see you here," he said. "And Anna, I wish to thank you for bringing the boy today." He extended his right hand, saying: "Peter, you are in for a good show. Landgrave Friedrich II of Hesse-Kassel is here today, drilling some of the troops at the castle. You will see them marching around to his own direct orders. He enjoys conducting formation drills. That'll give you a chance to see various military unit movements, the marching, as well as some musket drills. That ought to give you a good idea of the various commands that are commonly used, and the precision with which the soldiers carry them out. These fellows are real sharp. That's why they were assigned to the Palace Guard Detachment. They spend most of their time at the palace in Kassel, particularly when the Landgrave takes up residence there to participate in ceremonial exercises or whenever he receives special guests and foreign dignitaries. When the Landgrave is not in the area, or if he is preoccupied, one of the officers is responsible for drilling the troops.

"Let's walk over to the drill site near the ramparts at the far side of the castle and take a look. After that, we can probably join the troops as they eat their lunch. We'll see where we go from there. A lot depends on how much time we have left. I understand that brother Franz will want to pick you up sometime around four in the afternoon."

Mama said: "Karl, I am sure Peter will enjoy himself tremendously, every minute of it. You know, this may well become the most memorable day in his young life. He is forever talking about you and your regiment."

I was overwhelmed at how much my parents wanted to make

this a happy day for me. They sure knew how to do it, and I loved them both for it.

On our way, I noticed how sturdy the castle was built, constructed almost exclusively of solid granite blocks that were too heavy for an individual to lift, never mind carry. Papa said it must have taken many years to build such a complicated structure, especially to haul the building blocks uphill from down in the river valley. The outside walls were designed to be extra strong, thick enough to withstand any prolonged bombardment. Internally, there were many more walls, hallways, ramps and rooms, making this an exceptionally large castle. Papa went on to say that Marburg Castle had a very large ballroom, big enough for the Landgrave to drill his soldiers during inclement weather.

While heading for the drill site, father explained some of the castle's special features, pointing out the canons along the way and the cannonballs that had been neatly stacked nearby. Mother seemed even more amazed at what she was seeing. This was the first time she had ever been inside a castle. As we were about to turn another corner, Papa said: "O.K., just around the corner you will be standing one level above the drill area. The Landgrave may be in the yard below with a detachment of 50 or so soldiers, doing what he likes best, commanding them as they march about following his orders. I suggest we stand silently and watch so we don't interrupt the activities. When we have seen enough, I will give you a nudge, Anna, and you then tap Peter on the shoulder. That's when we will leave quietly."

Oh, how exciting it was to see the soldiers from above as they marched in columns of threes, making turns, changing direction, halting and doing some exercises with their muskets. Then they did all kinds of movements with their muskets while they were standing at attention, all the while the Landgrave was shouting out orders. He must be getting a sore throat after all that yelling, I thought.

We hadn't realized that Landgrave Friedrich had noticed our presence, even though we had been as quiet as mice. At one point, he looked up to where we were standing behind a stone railing, and called to Father:

"Sergeant Bauer, bring your boy down here and we'll let him

march along."

I suddenly got the jitters and was afraid to go, but my father said it was a great honor to be invited by the Landgrave, especially after we had just dropped by unannounced. As much as I wanted to march about like a soldier, it scared me to have to walk up to the Landgrave. To me, he was so high above our standing, that it seemed almost unreal to be entering his presence. But he knew Father from the days he had taken care of his horses at the estate, and later as one of his soldiers. Having most recently been promoted to sergeant made my father sort of a household item, I thought.

We reached the parade area as the soldiers were standing at ease, and walked over to the Landgrave. Father gave him a snappy salute. The Landgrave nodded his head in approval.

"Your Excellency, this is my son, Peter. He is so enthused about soldiers that I wanted to show him firsthand what soldiering is all about."

"You did well to bring him here. This is the right place, young Master Peter. Why don't you march alongside the soldiers, but keep a few feet away. I wouldn't want them to trample all over you when they suddenly change directions. So, stand over there and

listen to my commands. All you have to do is follow my orders and you'll be all right."

I glanced at my father quickly. He smiled at me and then stepped away from the drilling unit.

The Landgrave shouted: "Achtung. Stillgestanden," as the men came to attention.

I did the same, standing there, stiff as a board. He then ordered, "Links um," and I did a left face as the others did. Next, he ordered: "Vorwärts marsch," and I started to march forward, following the others. As the column reached the end of the yard, he shouted, "Linksschwenkt marsch," and the column made a left turn while marching. A few steps later, he repeated the order and we kept marching until we were about even with his position. He then shouted, "Abteilung halt!" and everyone stopped instantaneously. Again came the "Links um" order, and we all stood there facing him. He congratulated me for a job well done, and continued, "Come again, one day. Next time you can stand in the ranks with the soldiers. In the meantime, continue to be an honor to your family. Good day."

I thanked him somewhat meekly. "Danke sehr, Herr Landgraf," and walked to the side of the drill area where my father was still standing. He smiled, saying, "You did good. How did you like marching like a soldier?"

"Well, Papa, they were taking such big steps, I had a hard time keeping up with them while trying to listen for any new commands that might be given."

"Oh well," he said, "You would get used to the pace very quickly, I am sure."

We then returned to where Mother was waiting. She, too, was full of praises about how well I had done. She had been able to see everything from the floor above, where she had been standing all the time.

She said, "The soldiers marched in perfect step, and you, son, were just as good. You ought to be proud of yourself. Just imagine, you marched before the Landgrave in person; that's something no other young person in Kirchdorf has ever done. Remember this moment well."

Father then walked us to one of the smaller halls that had

been set aside as a dining facility for the troops. Altogether, there were about 120 soldiers mulling about, picking up their daily noontime rations, while others were eating, talking, laughing and still others, disposing of scraps and leftovers on their way out, heading back to their barracks rooms. I was surprised that they were all being fed from a central field kitchen area that was set up at one end of the hall. The stew they served had been good and tasty. I asked my father, "Do the soldiers always get fed by a central kitchen crew, like here?"

"No," he replied, "in the field, every four to six soldiers draw their daily food rations from the quartermaster and then as a group, they build a fire to do their own cooking. Sometimes they do a good job, and then there are times when they could have done better. That's what army life is about. You have to do whatever it takes to conform, blend in and survive whatever hardships may come your way."

We walked through the barracks area while the soldiers were elsewhere, carrying out their assigned duties for the day. I saw cots and hammocks with blankets placed on them; also, wooden boxes in which soldiers kept their belongings. Altogether, the place was neat and clean. However, I'd rather sleep in my own bed on the farm.

As we approached the orderly room, Papa said, "Let's see if my captain is in. I'd like to introduce the two of you."

Captain Albert von Schwetzingen was there.

Papa saluted him, saying: "Captain, I'd like you to meet my wife, Anna, and my son, Peter, whom we have been showing around today."

"Very nice, I am happy to meet you both. I hope you are having an enjoyable time at Marburg Castle. Sergeant, I seem to remember you asking about possibilities for your son becoming a drummer. In all sincerity, I'd like our youngest boys to be at least 10 years old. How old are you, Master Peter?"

"Sir, I will be 10 in a few months", I replied.

"That sounds good. Sergeant, why don't you draw sufficient material for a uniform from the quartermaster and perhaps Frau Anna can start making the uniform. You are a seamstress, are you not? I believe Sergeant Bauer mentioned that not too long ago."

"Oh yes, Captain von Schwetzingen, I'd be delighted to make a uniform for my son. It should definitely be done by his next birthday."

"Very well", the captain replied,

"Perhaps we'll have a new drummer in a few months. Oh, be sure you add the 'Schwalbennester,' the swallows' nests at the shoulders of his uniform, signifying he's a member of the music corps. We'll take care of all the formalities when the time comes."

Father then excused himself and his little entourage from the captain, thanking him for his kindness. We then left, heading for the supply room to look up Quartermaster Lieutenant Alfred Schmitt. On our arrival, Papa introduced us to the lieutenant, telling him of the discussion he had with Captain von Schwetzingen, and his wish that a uniform be made for Master Peter.

The lieutenant looked at me, saying: "And you are looking to become a drummer? Good luck. We have enough material to make a uniform. Let me pull it together and your family can take it with them."

He disappeared into another room in which I saw all kinds of things lined up and stacked. That seemed to be the storage facility for the supply room. We didn't have to wait long before the lieutenant returned with an armful of uniform cloth, in blue, white and black.

"That ought to do it," he said, as he dropped it on a table so Mother could look it over.

"Looks good to me," she said. "We'll get working on it. The next time we come to Marburg, we'll hopefully be able to show you a uniform, lieutenant."

"I'll be looking forward to seeing how you do," he replied.

By that time, it was getting close to four o'clock, and we headed for the gate. Papa bid us farewell when he noticed his brother, Franz, waiting outside, his wagon loaded with supplies. After hugs and kisses, we all went our different ways.

Mobilization

Papa came home for one day at Christmas in 1775. Although we enjoyed the season, including a nice snowfall that provided us with a great opportunity to take the sleigh from Opa's farm and go for a long and enjoyable sleigh ride through open country, Papa's mood was somewhat somber. He was quiet this time. In the past, he had been relaxed and talkative. On Christmas Eve, we followed the family tradition of pouring molten lead into a pan of cold water to see what the resulting lead shapes and designs might tell us of our coming year. We each had a turn at it and it was lots of fun. However, no matter how hard we tried to decipher the lead shapes and put some kind of meaning to them, nothing seemed to make any real sense. Papa's pouring came out like a porous glob of metal that showed some figures, maybe even some boats among a lot of nothing. Mother must have poured her lead very slowly, for in the bottom of the pan were an endless number of very small lead deposits that just couldn't be deciphered. I dropped my lead into the water the way my father had done, all at once. A cloud of steam rose from the pot, and in the water was a maze of lead strings going every which way. Papa said, "Well, it seems you'll be going in several directions this year, but I don't know what it means. Let's talk about it next year, maybe we'll experience something during the coming months that will help us figure it all out."

Finally, after a special Christmas dinner of goose, potato balls and red cabbage, father spoke up and told us what was bothering him. He said, "It is definite that an envoy of Britain's King George

III will be visiting the Landgrave at his palace in Kassel. They will seriously discuss a possible contribution of troops from Hesse-Kassel to help put down what has by now developed into a rebellion by the colonists in North America. I spoke to you of such a possibility the last time I was home, but I felt that our involvement may never happen. From what I can tell, our Landgrave is ready to support the British, remembering their earlier close alliance during the 12-year war.

"This didn't set very well with me. I am a soldier and I will do my duty, of course, but I do not wish to leave the two of you behind if at all possible, nor do I want to put you in harm's way.

"Because of the uncertainty of not knowing what's best for all of us, I have been withdrawn, just thinking and thinking. I have not come up with any solution."

At that point, Mother let him know that it was her impression that the three of us would go, if he could obtain permission to bring his family. She recounted that he had asked about her abilities and willingness to work as a seamstress for the troops, and perhaps as a nurse's assistant, if need arose. She added that she could also help as a teacher for the children others might bring. And as related to Peter, she was in the process of making his drummer uniform. That in itself should be enough to realize the boy was all fired up about going to America.

Papa took it all in and after a while said, "All right, if push comes to shove, and it is definite that we Hessians will indeed be dispatched to assist the British in restoring order in their colonies overseas, then I will officially ask to take my family with me. Now, one more time, Anna and Peter, would I be doing the right thing to ask for permission to bring you along?"

Mother and I both responded in the affirmative. Shortly after, father returned to Marburg.

On January 15, 1776, Colonel William Faucett, empowered to act on behalf of King George III of Britain, met with Landgrave Friedrich II of Hesse-Kassel to work out a contract acceptable to both sides. It envisioned Hesse to initially provide some 12,500 soldiers and officers for overseas duty. In turn, they agreed on certain attractive financial arrangements satisfactory to the Landgrave. Each year, he would receive an acceptable amount for each soldier made available to the King. A special fee would also be paid to the Landgrave for every Hessian soldier wounded or killed, and British paymasters overseas were to cover the Hessian payrolls and other authorized expenses within the terms of the contract. It was also agreed that Hessian troops abroad would be responsible to their own officers, including top-ranking Hessian Generals operating under the overall command of their British sponsor. Due to the soldiers' dual sponsorships, they would be required to give an oath of allegiance to the King of England prior to departing for North America, in addition to the oath they had previously given to their Landgrave.

Immediately after signing the contracts, 14 regiments and seven battalions located at various locations within the principality of Hesse were given official orders advising them to prepare to move out in relays commencing on February 11, with the last unit not moving out until April 1776. It was estimated that some regiments would require up to six weeks to march to their designated North Sea port of embarkation. There, they would board ships initially bound for England, where they could be required to transfer to larger ocean-going ships and sail as a convoy to North America.

Within hours of receiving his mobilization orders, Colonel von Ditfurth assembled his officers for an initial briefing, after which they relayed the information to their own units stationed at various locations within the Hesse-Kassel region. Captain von Schwetzingen summoned Sergeants Meyer, Weinfeld and Bauer to his office, where he advised them that the colonel had approved their respective families to accompany the regiment when it moved out, suggesting they be notified immediately so they can begin preparing for the journey that was being scheduled in relays. He emphasized that the Ditfurth Regiment had been tagged to be the first unit to leave Marburg on February 11, 1776. That was within a very short period of three weeks.

Sergeant Bauer requested a 12-hour pass and permission to requisition a regimental horse so he could dash out to Kirchdorf to alert his family and return in time for the morning formation. The captain approved his request promptly, saying, "Sergeant

Bauer, you might ask your wife to expedite making your son's uniform. We have a very long march ahead of us and could use a few relief drummers, even if not yet formally enrolled. Besides, it would be good training for the boy, and an occasional missed drumbeat would hardly be noticed. I envision that many of our troops will be exhausted from the exceptionally long hikes that we expect, so many won't be paying much attention to the drumbeats, anyway."

Papa then galloped all the way to the farm. His coming was unexpected, so when he raced into the yard, we were joyfully surprised. His horse was foaming from the mouth and he promptly took care of his faithful friend. While pumping a bucket of water from the well in the center of the farmyard, he called, "Anna, I could go for a piece of rye bread with liverwurst, and a cold beer to take away my own thirst."

"Right away, Karl. I'll set it up for you."

He continued, "Anna, please call our family together, Opa included. I have some important information to share with all of you and I have to head back at four o'clock in the morning."

"Yes, Karl," Anna replied. "Do you want young Peter there, too?"

"By all means, have him join us."

The family gathered in the farmhouse kitchen an hour later, Opa and Frank included. When everyone was seated, Papa began to speak:

"Well, it's official, we are being mobilized as part of a Hesse-Kassel army of some 12,500 soldiers, whom the Landgrave has committed to serve King George III of Britain, in North America. In fact, our regiment has orders to move out on February 11, just three weeks from now. That doesn't give anyone much time. It is important to remember that Anna and Peter will also be going. The regiment has approved their status as accompanying dependents. Pa, this means they will not be here to help on the farm until we all return. And Frank, my dear brother, you may have to hire another permanent hand to assist you, for I am aware of just how hard Anna has been working on the farm, and that she could always be counted on to make things happen," he said. "The

developments, though a part of a soldier's duties, are somewhat unusual in that the Landgrave is letting 12,500 men of his army of 16,000, serve England, leaving a mere 3,500 soldiers at home, tasked with protecting all of Hesse-Kassel. I know he will have to implement his recruiting edicts of 1762 pretty quickly to begin training new recruits to fill the gaps being left by the departing units."

"And now, son, my captain has expressed his hopes that your mother will be able to sew up a uniform for you, before the two of you depart on our cross-country convoy. He wants to get you started even though you are not quite 10 years old. He is confident that you will have chances to practice the basic drumbeats while en route to our designated port of embarkation. That pretty much does it. I'll let you know, Anna, what to pack as soon as I am provided more definite information."

We were all shocked at the short deadline we were given to get ready for such a long and perhaps prolonged journey. Papa spoke again, telling us, "From the time you leave Kirchdorf, it could take four or more months before you set foot on the American continent. There is no way to predict what things will be like by then. So it behooves us to do our best to get there as fast as possible to stop the unrest. We just can't tell what we will encounter until we are there."

Opa listened attentively; for the most part, he was silent and withdrawn. He was thinking, perhaps, about how best to handle the farm in the future. Until then, he had depended and relied on his closest family members to tackle the toughest jobs and to supervise the hired help. While he and Franz had always worked well together, the time had come for them to work even closer. Franz let it be known that he was confident the two of them would be able to manage the farm until Karl and his family returned.

Mother, who had always been the calm one in the family, had a worried look on her face. Perhaps not even Papa realized just how great a burden was being placed on her shoulders to handle the preparations for their move, and without causing any last-minute hang-ups. To top it off, she had been asked to make my uniform during the same three weeks she had to get ready for the trip. It seemed a bit unfair to her. As for myself, I started to beat out marching rhythms with my fingers whenever I sat at a table. Mother thought I was getting nervous, but I kept telling her that I just wanted to stay ahead of the happenings. I wouldn't want to fail my first real drum exercise, should there be one when we assembled at the castle in Marburg. 'Til then, I wouldn't even see a drum, never mind know how to use one, and in a formation, that gave me the jitters. It was all a bit scary to me when I thought about it, but I couldn't let on and give her any more headaches than she already had.

Papa rode out of the farm gate at 4 o'clock sharp, even before the rooster crowed. By the time we were up and sitting around the breakfast table, he would have been back at his duty station. A mere two days later, he paid us another unannounced visit, this time providing us with the information we needed to pack up, get ready and head to Marburg on February 10, where we were to spend the night, ready to move out with the troops the following morning.

CHAPTER 8

The Long Hike

When we arrived at the castle late in the afternoon on February 10, our wagon, driven by Uncle Franz, was directed to the area where we had observed soldiers drilling during a prior visit. Several young soldiers were waiting, ready to unload our baggage and transfer our belongings to a waiting regimental wagon. Uncle Franz said his last farewells, wishing both of us the best of luck and health, and then headed back to the farm.

On leaving, he said, "Tell brother Karl to keep his head down. We want him back in one piece; we need him. Be sure you tell him that. Also, I wish all of you God speed."

We didn't realize until he had left that it could be a long time before we saw him and Opa again. It was a sad moment, but one which we could not dwell on for too long.

An orderly came and asked us to follow him to our accommodations for the night. Other military personnel had already taken several of the bunks that had been set up in a large hall, but we were able to find two bunks close to each other. We didn't mind a little inconvenience. It was only for one night. A short while later, Papa showed up. His uniform was damp from perspiration and he was wiping the sweat on his brow.

"This has been a hectic day for all of us here at the castle," he said. "But we finally have everything lined up, ready to roll in the morning. I am glad you're settled in. Let's get a bite to eat and pick up your dry rations for the morning. And don't forget, between 5 and 6 o'clock, you'll be able to have coffee and milk. We understand that the first wagons will get under way no later than seven o'clock. I may not be with you when the column moves out, but don't get worried, just follow the instructions you are given. I have been assured that both of you will be assigned to the same wagon. I am sure to catch up with you later in the morning. By the way, Peter, I have packed a drum for you in our supply wagon, so you'll be able to do some rhythm exercises along the way. Be patient."

As tired as we were, we slept soundly until 4 o'clock, when Sergeant Meyer let it be known with a loud voice that it was time to get up. After he made sure that most of the civilians were at least sitting in their bunks, or rubbing their eyes, he shouted so everyone could hear, "Good morning, fellow travelers. I hope you had a restful night sleeping barracks style, the way soldiers do it all the time. This will be a busy day for you. Morning coffee and milk will be available in this hall in an hour. In the meantime, I suggest you wash and dress, then bring your morning rations with you and go to the far end of the hall to eat and have your coffee. The rations given to you last night included bread, cheese and a piece of smoked bratwurst. I know, because I am with the quartermaster. So, enjoy your first military meal while you anticipate what comes next. You will be mounting your respective wagons no later than 6:30. Here are your assignments: Anna and Peter Bauer will travel in wagon number 10; Bertha, Fritz and Martha Meyer will go to wagon number 11; and the Weinfelds, consisting of Lotte, Margarite and Elizabeth; will find room on wagon 12. For your information, the wagons are loaded with regimental supplies of all sorts. You will find your own bags in the wagon to which you have been assigned. You are to remain in the wagon as the column makes its way through the town of Marburg. Somewhere outside of the town limits, you will be told when you can get off and walk, if you wish. A bit of exercise shouldn't hurt anyone. Any questions? None. Okay, time to get moving. See you all later." With that, he walked over to his family, gave them each a hug and he left.

We had to hustle to clean up and dress, and then head to the end of the hall for breakfast. The milk tasted good. It had been chilled, the way I liked it.

I could tell that Mother was enjoying her first cup of coffee the way she did at home every morning. She said "hello" to Sergeants Meyer and Weinfeld's family members. I looked around for people my age, but there were none, just girls and a boy who was maybe five years old. Even if it probably wouldn't be any fun, I thought we would all be seeing a lot of each other along the trek and maybe even after we got to the colonies.

As we left the hall, the narrow passages within the castle were badly congested, almost impassable. There were wagons, people and soldiers all over the place. We stood a moment to watch and take it all in. Neither of us had ever seen such a crowd. As we were walking toward the outer courtyard to locate wagon number 10, we saw more than 100 soldiers lined up. Papa was with them. He was sizing the soldiers up, pointing to things here and there, like the soldier who was wearing his tall headdress crooked, and one who hadn't buttoned his gaiters completely. We soon spotted our wagon and while we were standing, waiting, we heard military commands from the direction we had come from. That must be Papa's unit. Then, suddenly, there was the sound of drums. Oh, how excited I was.

"Mother, do you hear that, there must be at least two drummers with them. I hope they come marching past us."

"It seems they will, Peter. I can see them entering the courtyard."

Then I could hear: "Thump, thump, thump-thump-thump."

"Wow, look at them, they are real neat. And all are in perfect step. There's Papa, see him, Ma?" I waved and yelled: "Hi Papa, hi Papa," but he didn't hear me.

As the soldiers came closer, the drummers changed their rhythm. Now it was more like "varoom-boom-boom, varoom-boom-boom," and the soldiers were marching faster. They had changed their pace, following the beat of the two drummers who were marching at the head of the column. As I saw all this, I could envision myself in their place. Oh, how exciting. I hoped they would let me march with the soldiers soon.

The troops positioned themselves at the head of the wagon train by marching through the portal of the castle and part way down the path toward town. A few minutes later, the order, "Move out," was shouted from the front and repeated again and again along the entire length of the column, until the last people in the back had heard the command. The drummers started up again and the wagons began moving, each jerking forward as the horses were set in motion.

We had reached the bottom of the hill and were merging into the first Marburg street by the time the last wagon cleared the portal at the castle. It was a long line. The ride was bumpy as the loaded wagons made their way along the cobblestone streets, much like the times when Opa or Uncle Franz took me to town to deliver or pick up supplies. The column moved slowly. The towns-people saw a long procession. Many of them lined the streets, waving. They had seen marching soldiers from time to time, but never anything like this. They must have thought the regiment was leaving, lock, stock and barrel, but not so; there were still several hundred soldiers at the castle or at a nearby barracks area. Father had said the column would be picking up another 500 men or so as we passed through their garrison towns. These soldiers would belong to another of the Landgrave's regiments.

What I didn't realize was that the regiment had its own band of musicians, and that they were waiting for us in front of the Town Hall, where Colonel von Ditfurth, his top staff officers and several local dignitaries would observe the regiment as it paraded past the reviewing stand. Wait 'til they see the long procession of all those horses and wagons, I thought. They would surely be tired by the time it was over.

As our wagon neared the site, we could hear the band. I got goosebumps; it was so touching. All I could imagine was being their drum major, the tambour I wanted to be so badly. They were playing stirring marching music, the kind Frederick the Great would order when he went to special events. Up front were the soldiers of Papa's unit. They marched proudly in perfect procession as they paraded in front of the dignitaries. My father must have been delighted with their performance. From what I could tell from standing in the moving wagon, though farther back in the line, they looked great. Next was our column of rattling and creaking horse-drawn wagons, followed by a well-outfitted detail of horsemen on their mounts, then more wagons and at the end, another large contingent of some 200 soldiers, or more. They provided a perfect conclusion to the special procession.

Meanwhile, local civilians stood waving and shouting friendly farewells, especially near the Town Hall. If anyone felt low on that day, the enthusiasm of the people, the cheering and well wishing, the marching music, and the salutes offered from the reviewing stand by the dignitaries would have without doubt lifted their spirits. The realization that the troops' participation in the overseas campaign would bring honor and respect to Landgrave Friedrich II, and the principality of Hesse-Kassel as a whole, would have quickly replaced whatever negative thoughts anyone

may have had.

After we left Marburg and traveled along country roads for several hours, orders were given to halt the wagons and allow anyone wishing to walk for a while to dismount. Mother and I got off and began walking alongside our wagon. By mid-afternoon, we reached another village and, to our surprise, the regimental cooks had set up a field kitchen in the village square ahead of time. They had prepared a caldron of hearty potato soup that was ready and waiting. We were quite hungry by then, and got ourselves a good helping, along with bread and butter. Fresh water, which the local farmers provided, was standing in large buckets, waiting for us to help ourselves.

As soon as everyone had eaten, the convoy got underway again. We were still walking instead of riding in the wagon, but it was a chore to keep up with the column, which was actually picking up speed. We found out that the objective was to reach a larger village before dark. When we arrived, the soldiers were ordered to pitch their tents on a meadow nearest to the village, while the civilians, my mother and I included, were invited to eat with some of the local farm families and remain with them overnight. That was unexpected, and a very kind gesture of the people in that village.

Just imagine, strangers being invited to stay overnight at another family's home. Papa caught up with us about then and asked, "How are you two making out? Anna, is the wagon okay? I hope you can rearrange things in the back so you can sleep en route, or find a spot to sit that's soft enough while we are trekking along. This is a very long haul. I know that, and I am proud of both of you. You can always get hold of me. I'll be with my company most of the time and we'll be the first unit up front, ahead of the wagons. The commander let us know that we will have to pick up speed if we are to arrive at our port on the North Sea by the date the British want us there. We must be in time to sail for England and meet their convoy to North America. That means, if you elect to walk, it may become strenuous if you try to keep it up too long. I suggest you switch a bit between walking and riding. Peter, I will try to dig out the drum from the supply wagon. If I can manage, I'll bring it to you in a day or so. Being so far back in the column, your drumbeats would not interfere with the drummers up front

with my company. So, you could actually be practicing the basic rhythm beats as you walk alongside the wagons. By doing so, you'll soon be marching instead of walking, just as I did when I first signed up. But remember, you cannot officially become a drummer until you are 10. You'll be in North America by then. Thus, use the time you have now to get the hang of things. Enough for tonight, I'll see you both at your wagon in the morning. We march at 6 o'clock. Have a good night. God be with you."

We slept well in our feather beds. The farmer's wife, Frau Ellen, cooked some boiled eggs for breakfast, plus a few extras to take with us. She also packed some bread and a hunk of cheese, not knowing what arrangements had been made for us on the following day. We ate well and Mother had her coffee for the day. The farmer gave me some juice from squeezed berries his family had picked the day before we arrived. It was delicious. I ought to ask Opa to plant some berry bushes when we get back. I was sure he would do it for me.

In the morning, as we were climbing up on our wagon, Papa dropped by to inquire about our night at the farmer's house, and to wish us well on the day's journey. Mother told him we had enjoyed the stay and had been treated like family friends. Staying and eating at a farm was like being back in Kirchdorf. He was pleased with our positive feedback. I know he must be worrying about us, in addition to his many military responsibilities. Soon the wagon train got under way, and for the first few hours, we

relaxed in the wagon while enjoying the countryside and the beautiful scenery we had not seen before. Our routine was much like the day before. We stopped to eat and take a break, walked a while, found a new village in which to settle down for the night, and the following morning we were off again. We marched through the towns of Treysa and Zsiegenhain, where other units of our regiment were stationed. Word got around that they would be moving out the following week to avoid any congestion on the roads north.

Upon our arrival in Kassel, the official seat of our Landgrave, another parade had been arranged. This one turned out to be much bigger than the one in Marburg, with lots more pomp. The streets were lined and cordoned off by the soldiers stationed in Kassel, along with members of other nearby regiments who had been summoned to Kassel for the event. That night, when it was all over and before we were quartered with one of the families in town, Papa caught up with us once again. "Wasn't that a fantastic showing?" he asked. "The Landgrave was delighted, I was told. And did you notice he sat astride Mamatschi when he reviewed the parade? I found myself smiling when I caught a glance of the horse as we passed in review. The Landgrave must have noticed, because he smiled back and had Matamtschi raise her front right hoof in salute. I'm telling you, for me this was one of the most memorable moments since I've been in the Landgrave's service." As usual, Papa bid us good night and wished us a pleasant day. Then, he headed back to be with his soldiers.

Eventually, we reached the Weser River, where we were told our column would continue its trek over land, whereas the troops following us in the coming week, would be transported to Bremerlehe by way of a small flotilla of river boats. The next few days were without any special events as we followed the river northward. Then came an unexpected two full days of thunder, lightning and cloud bursts. The rain was so intense that we had to button down our tarpaulins tightly to stay dry inside the wagon. We couldn't tell whether it was day or night; that it was a time for sleeping or just trying, amid all the noise nature was exposing us to. Though covered with a tarpaulin, the two soldiers sitting outside on the driver's seat trying to keep the horses in check were soaked and wet to the bones. The driving rain was unbelievable. When it was over, we learned that the horses on one of the rigs had gone wild, taking off as runaways. They supposedly ran uncontrollably across an open meadow and straight into the river, where the wagon sank with the horses still hitched up.

After the storm, Papa stopped by to see if we were okay. His hands were bandaged. Almost in unison, we said, "What happened to you?"

"During the height of the storm, my horses shied during the loud thunder and lightning, and ran off so fast we couldn't stop them. Two of my men and I fell off the rig as the horses went off the road, galloping across a meadow and into the water. Luckily, none of us were badly hurt, but we did lose the wagon and both horses. The wagon had been loaded with 12 new tents. The weight of the cargo just pulled it under in the swiftly moving water and it disappeared. Peter, I am sorry to have to tell you that the drum I had scrounged up for you was on the wagon when it went down."

I was saddened and ready to cry, when Papa continued.

"Don't worry, we'll find another one, but it may take a while. I'll have to check with the other regiments after we get to the port, maybe one of them brought an extra that we could borrow until you get your own after your birthday. Keep smiling, you'll do all right."

The next day or two were boring for me. Mother was sitting on the driver's bench most of the time, sewing something and chatting with the soldier holding the reins. I was on the ground walking and kicking stones. My feet hurt, and I had blisters. I was actually limping. Everything had become uncomfortable. Besides, they sped up the marching tempo and made it even harder for me to keep up the longer we were on the road. Several times, I jumped on the back of the moving wagon, which I had been told not to do. But I couldn't wait for the convoy to stop; my feet hurt too much. I sat in the back, brooding. All I could think of was that everything had gone wrong. I couldn't sign up as a drummer yet because I hadn't reached my tenth birthday, Papa had lost my drum when his wagon went into the river, and my mother wasn't paying any attention to me. She was always sewing. And my feet were a mess and I could hardly walk.

For the overnight stop, we camped in a meadow along the river. I used that opportunity to skip down to the cold water, where I soaked my feet. Although they were numb, all the pain went away. I felt a lot better. I looked around and decided to throw stones at some of the passing flotsam. Along the edge of the water, not too far downstream from where I was sitting, I noticed an object that was caught in some branches of overhanging shrubbery. Curiosity prompted me to take a closer look. As I reached the spot, I couldn't believe my eyes. It was my drum! I was so excited, I jumped into the water and pulled it free. After managing to get it on land, I realized all I had was the bare drum. The skins were missing from both ends, and the tension ropes were gone. But even though the drum had been in the water for several days, it looked pretty good, and it wasn't warped. Of course, it would need fixing and painting. Only after making the assessment did I realize that my clothes were soaking wet. It was getting dark and I needed to change, so I grabbed the skeleton of my drum and hastened to our wagon.

My parents were there, talking. I shouted, "Papa, look what I found. My drum!"

"Where in the world did you find it?" he asked. "It looks like it's been waterlogged."

"It was caught in the bushes down by the river. It can be repaired, can't it?"

"To me it looks like a casualty, but I will take it with me and show it to our wagon master. He is a highly skilled tradesman and knows his way around with the various types of wood. If it can be fixed, I know he'll do it for me. He could probably even make the wooden rings that hold the hides at each end. Anna, I think I'll head back down the line right now. Maybe I can get hold of the wagon master before nightfall and see what he might have to say about rebuilding the drum."

"That's fine, Karl, I am happy you were able to spend some time with me. Hopefully, we will see more of each other after we leave on the British transports. By the way, how much longer will it be before we reach Bremerlehe?"

"It shouldn't take more than two or three more days. Then, of course, we'll be in the hands of our sponsors, the British. I don't know how fast they will move us along. I imagine they will arrange stocking the ships with sufficient supplies that will last until we reach their port of Portsmouth. Besides, other columns of soldiers following us have to board ships and sail from Bremerlehe when we do. So there could be some delay before we can board the ships. But Anna, broadly speaking, it ought not take much longer before you can get off your wagon for the night. Take care." He then returned to his unit.

CHAPTER 9

Embarkation

We learned the following day that my father had spoken with the wagon master, who felt he could rebuild the drum, but he did not have any wood pieces flexible enough to make the rings that hold the top and bottom drum surfaces. He most likely wouldn't be able to obtain what he needed until the regiment arrived in England, or perhaps not even before we landed in North America. Papa told us again that he would continue trying some of the other Ditfurth units, and even other regiments at the staging area, to see if one of them could make a drum available on a loan basis. Aside from that, I couldn't do much but wait.

After three more grueling and long days en route to our embarkation point, we were finally told that we were approaching the staging area the British had set up to receive our long convoy. At that point, we had been underway for 40 days, a whole six weeks. About an hour later, the wagon train and the military units came to a halt. The civilians riding in the conveyances remained in their places, while the troops, except for the wagon drivers, assembled at the head of the line. Following a routine head count by British personnel, they proceeded to walk the length of the standing wagons to obtain their own count of the teams and horses they would have to stow aboard the waiting ships. When done, our convoy commander moved his personnel and supplies further into the enclave and closer to our designated dock. As we inched forward, the column was reformed into a column of three wagons abreast to shorten the overall length of the column, and to consolidate the supplies and their conveyances in a smaller area at dockside.

Lieutenant Schmitt, the supply officer, conferred repeatedly with Sergeant Meyer, primarily to identify which wagons and supplies would be loaded aboard specific ships earmarked for our regiment, at least for those elements that were already in the staging area. Mother and I stayed in our wagon for several hours until the word came to dismount. We then headed to one of the large stone buildings for our meals and to be assigned sleeping spaces for the next few nights.

As we were eating, this time bratwurst and sauerkraut with applesauce, we saw my father at the far end of the messing facility. He was speaking with an officer from another regiment. I could tell by the uniform the officer was wearing; it was a bit different than his. I wondered if he was asking about a drum. I guess that's all I had been thinking about for the last few days. To top it off, I was getting nervous. I needed to practice aboard ship so I could at least learn the most basic drumbeats by the time we reached America.

We were enjoying the food when Papa came by our table.

"Hello, again. I see you are eating well; just like home, isn't it? Eat enough while you can. I hear it won't be as good aboard ship. We'll probably have a few slow days until the next wagon train with more troops arrives. So partake of the meals served here at the embarkation center, and fill your bellies.

"I was just speaking with an officer from the Prinz Carl Regiment of Hersfeld. He has been here with an advance party from his regiment for the past week, arranging for their arrival. I asked if he could let me know if his supply people brought an extra drum with them. He said he would be delighted to find out. You know, Peter, I am spending more time trying to replace your drum than I am with my men. But don't worry, my priorities are and must remain those of my military assignments. Nevertheless, I would personally like to see you with a drum. Let's hope it all works out. Anna, Peter mentioned the last time I spoke with him that you were always busy sewing. Anything special?"

"Well, I didn't want to talk about it yet, but since you asked, I have been sewing Peter's uniform. I never had time to start before we left home. It's coming along slowly, but fine."

I jumped with joy when I heard what she said.

"Oh, Mother, I'm so sorry to have complained about your lack of attention to me, when all along I was receiving all of your attention without realizing it. Shame on me. I apologize."

"That's all right, Peter. If all goes well, I'll finish it on board the transport while at sea."

"Well, boy, never underestimate your mother. She never forgets a thing. She sets her priorities. With her, it's first things first. I guess right now, the uniform is the most important thing on her list. Take a walk around the docks in the morning. There are about 30 ships out there ready to tie up and take on their cargo when given the order to do so. I'll probably see you while you are out there exploring. Note the different uniforms the soldiers are wearing. They are from several other regiments that will be shipping out with us. Pay attention, you can learn a lot just being alert and keeping a watchful eye. All right, you two, I'm off to the troop quarters for the night. You should each have a blanket on your assigned bunk. Ha, this time it's straw you'll be sleeping on, not featherbeds. You are beginning to live like soldiers sooner than I thought. Take care. Have a good night."

After he left, mother and I picked up our bunk assignments. The orderly directed us to a smaller room, where some of the other civilians had already settled in for the night. It didn't take long to fall asleep, except that someone was snoring so loudly, it kept spoiling my dreams. Mother also woke up several times during the night, hemming and hawing. It must have been about three in the morning before I finally dozed off for good. At 5 o'clock, I heard the bugler sound the wake-up call for the troops. That put a final damper on my night's rest. Still quite sleepy, I stumbled to the washroom and got ready for the day. Some of the others were also milling around and getting dressed. Mother joined some of the other women when they went to an area set aside for them to clean up.

We enjoyed our breakfast of potato pancakes with fruit preserves. Mother's eyes lit up when she got her first cup of coffee for the day. I had a glass of cool milk, not really fresh, but cool. Afterwards, she said she wanted to do some more sewing, and that I could find her in the wagon standing near the dock if I needed her. I went for a stroll along the staging area as my father had suggested. Of course, she yelled after me, "You be careful now; don't go too close to the edge of the dock."

"Yes, Mother, I'll watch where I'm going," I replied, as I headed out the door.

When we pulled in, I hadn't noticed how large the staging area was. The dock was enormously long. Several transports were tied up, ready to accept their cargo, while others were anchored farther out, waiting. All I had seen before was the assembly area of our von Ditfurth Regiment. The wagons and equipment had been moved closer together during the night, and soldiers were posted as guards. Just past our area at dockside, the von Donop Regiment had arranged their wagons and gear, ready for loading aboard ship. Next to them, Regiment Du Corps had assembled its wagons and equipment in a similar manner. A few more units had staged their property even farther down the line.

I noticed the horse teams were no longer with their wagons, so I asked one of the guards about them. He said, "On arrival, the horses were sheltered in the large warehouse across from the dock, where they are being cared for. When it's time to load the ships, the horses will be taken aboard by their regiments and lowered into one of the holds prepared to receive them, along with their loaded hay wagons. Aboard ship, they will be cared for by their own handlers. I feel sorry for the horses. Those poor animals will have to remain tied up for the duration of the trip without ever being able to see much daylight, never mind running free in a pasture. I guess we won't have it much better, I mean the troops and you folks. We are all going to be stuck aboard our ships for several months, they tell me. I'm not looking forward to that. What is there to do aboard ship? It'll get pretty boring after a while, I am sure. I packed a few nice pieces of wood in one of our wagons that I hope to use to whittle a set of figures for a chess game."

"Wow," I said, "do you know how to play chess? My father does. He's a sergeant in the von Ditfurth Regiment. I bet he'd play."

"Well, son. I'm pretty sure most of the Ditfurth people will be sailing aboard the ship that's tied up at the dock near your equipment. My regiment will most likely be traveling on the transport over there, next to our equipment. Oh well, maybe I'll meet him when we get to the other side. Anyway, I have a feeling they'll begin loading the cargo real soon. They can't afford having us sit around doing nothing, that's not the military way."

By the time I walked the entire length of the docks, I had passed the assembled cargo of six regiments. Just as I was about to head back, I saw soldiers hustling about, attaching ropes to several wagons while sailors on the ship docked next to the staged equipment were preparing booms to lift the cargo aboard. So, they are beginning to load, I thought. I better get back.

As I headed back, I saw the guard I had spoken with earlier. He was still on duty. As I approached, he smiled and said, "Well, young man, it won't be long now. Everyone is getting ready to load. My regiment will get started in another hour or so.

"I imagine your group will also be moving their cargo pretty soon. You are quite young to be experiencing this type of operation. This is the first time I have seen so many soldiers with their equipment assembled in one area, never mind being shipped across the ocean on a multitude of ships. There are so many of them out there, I've lost count. Tell me, how old are you anyway? You can't be older than nine or 10?"

"I'm going to be 10 in a few months; then I'll become a drummer," I said.

"Your father is taking a chance, bringing his family along."

"Well, my father is a sergeant, and he was given permission to take us along."

The guard smiled, shaking his head: "As a drummer boy, you'll have to keep your eyes open if you ever have to beat the drum during an engagement with the enemy. But I don't think there will be any serious fighting, anyway. Not after the colonists become aware of our numbers, and realize the King is determined to restore order in the colonies."

"That's what my father said," I replied.

The guard shook his head, and continued: "I hope that is the way it will be, but we have to be prepared for the worst. That's why I say: Be alert and watch everything that's going on around you, particularly if you find yourself at the head of a column marching toward the enemy."

"Well, sir, I thank you for telling me these things. I will remember what you said. But for now, I better get back to my mother; she's probably waiting and wondering where I am. She might even want me to try on the uniform she is making for me, so I best run along, now. Goodbye, sir."

The guard smiled and waved as I walked off.

When I reached our staging area, mother had returned to the building where we were housed. There were additional guards on duty. When asked, one of them told me the regiment had received notice to rig the wagons so they could be lifted onto the *Spring*, the transport tied up alongside our pier, and that all personnel should remain in their billeting areas during the ongoing loading operations. I could understand that. They wanted to be sure no one would get hurt while the heavy cargo items were being shifted around. So I headed for the large brick building, where I knew I'd find my mother.

I spotted her on the ground floor, sitting on a barrel along the wall where she was sewing, as usual. When she saw me, her face lit up.

"Where have you been? I worried about you. You have been gone for over three hours," she said.

"I checked out the docks as Papa suggested. Do you know there are at least six regiments in the staging area, and some have started loading their cargo? I also had a long talk with one of the guards along the way. He told me a lot about being alert all the time, especially as a drummer, marching ahead of the regiment," I replied.

"That made a lot of sense, but I could have told you the same. Did he scare you?"

"Not really," I said, "however, marching up front during an engagement with the enemy could be pretty risky. Still, he didn't think it would ever come to any fighting, just like Papa said."

"Well, son, during your absence I was urged to stay in our billets until we are called to board ship. You'll have to help me carry our belongings when it's time to go, so stay nearby. I will be taking the material and accessories for your uniform. Hopefully, I'll be able to finish up the uniform once we are on the ship."

"How far along are you?"

"Oh, the jacket has been assembled with rough stitching; it ought to look okay when it's done. The vest should not take too long. As for as the leotards, I can stitch them up pretty quickly, too. Actually, all I need is a week of uninterrupted sewing," she replied.

"Gee, I can't wait to try it on. Have you seen Papa yet?" I asked.

"No, the last I heard is that he's busy assigning his men to preparing the wagons for the lift aboard ship," she replied.

We then watched from one of the windows as the soldiers assembled near the regiment's cargo, where they received their assignments. Some were running about tying ropes to the wagons as sailors maneuvered the ship's booms into position for the ropes to be attached for the lift. Soon, the wagons were being hoisted aboard. Smaller bags were carried up the gangplank by sailors.

When we got in line to receive our evening meals, word was passed that we should be ready to board ship at 6 o'clock on the morning of April 17. That was good news. The long overland trek and the long wait in the staging area would finally be over. Then, we could contemplate the ocean and the unknown beyond.

Just as we were getting ourselves ready to board the ship in the morning, Papa stopped by for a moment to wish us well and tell us that he and his detachment of soldiers would be sailing on the *Spring* with us, along with additional Ditfurth personnel. The remainder of the regiment would sail aboard the second ship tied up at the dock.

At 6 o'clock sharp in the morning, a bugle sounded, telling us to gather near the gangplank at the dock. Sergeant Meyer of the quartermaster's staff was standing by, holding a list with the names of the people authorized to board the ship. He called out the names in alphabetical order. We were the first.

"Bauer, Anna and Bauer, Peter," he called.

Mother replied: "Here."

"Board the ship up the gangplank," he ordered, and we started up the steep incline to the upper deck. We could hear him calling out the names of his own family and the Weinfelds, as well as several workers, like the wagon master, wagon hands and tent hands. Once up the gangplank, a British naval person welcomed us aboard. After a group of our people had gathered, a deck hand escorted us to our spaces just below the upper deck. Oh my gosh, I thought, when I saw lots of hammocks hanging from beams all over the place, but there were also some wooden bunks with sacks of straw on them. The women were told to congregate in an area set aside for their use along an outer wall where the bunks were.

Being a boy, I was assigned a hammock in the section for men. I tried getting in it, but it flipped around every time I tried, with me landing on the hard deck. I'm glad no one was paying any attention to me. It was embarrassing not being able to get on a hammock. A sailor wearing a broad grin stopped as he was passing. He looked scary, with broken teeth showing when he laughed. I thought he looked real ugly. Besides, his clothes probably hadn't been washed in some time.

He said, "Come here, lad. Let me show you how it's done," and with a single jump, he was laying in the hammock, grinning.

"Now you try it," he said.

I did exactly what he had done and I propelled myself right into the hammock, as though I had done it many times before. I was real proud of myself.

"There you go," he said, "you'll make a good sailor one day. Good luck."

He disappeared as fast as he had appeared. I noticed several other sailors working around; all talking loudly and boisterously, some using foul language. I know my folks would never have allowed such talk back home.

I looked for my mother, but she seemed to have settled in, sitting on the edge of her bunk with our two bags of belongings by her side. She smiled at me.

"This ought to be exciting," she said.

"Yes, and I don't think I'm going to like it," I responded.

"Well, we both wanted to go with your father, so here we are – going with him. It ought to be getting better once we arrive in the colonies," she commented.

After a few hours, the ship got under way, moving first into the channel in the middle of the river. After setting sails, the *Spring* headed into the North Sea. Naval officers were shouting orders to the crew, and the sailors seemed busy with all kinds of chores, tightening ropes and climbing up into the crow's nest, while others were sweeping decks.

CHAPTER 10

"Ships Ahoy!"

While the *Spring* was slowly gliding into open waters, I looked back to catch a final glimpse of the mainland we were leaving behind. I was surprised to see that a line of eight enormous cargo ships, much like ours, were following us. They had formed a single line by the time the Weser River merged with the North Sea. That's when I remembered having seen these ships tied up along the wharf when I took my early morning walk a day or two before. They must have loaded their cargo at the same time the *Spring* was stowing our equipment. We had been so preoccupied with what was going on in our immediate vicinity that I hadn't paid much attention to anything else. Since these ships had left their loading points, I imagined the ships that were anchored in the middle of the river would have moved to the docks to receive their cargo when the next wagon train loaded with supplies and equipment arrived. There had been talk that several more regiments were due to assemble at the port soon after our departure.

April 17, 1776 was a bright and sunny day, with a cool and refreshing breeze blowing from across the salty sea. Under the circumstances, we felt we could finally relax. For us, the time of waiting in uncertainty, of hustling about and even sitting around waiting for something to happen seemed to be over. We were entering a time for new adventures, of sailing across an ocean that none of us, except the sailors, had ever experienced before. From this point on, our lives would be in the hands of the ship's captain, in whom we had no alternative but to place our trust.

I was always silently praying for a chance to practice on a drum, anyone's drum. I felt we might be in for a long and boring journey, and I couldn't help but wish that I were given the opportunity to prepare for my future assignment as a drummer boy before we reached the colonies. Looking up to the sky, I saw flocks of seagulls following the ships. Against a perfectly blue sky with scattered white clouds, the gulls were circling majestically above our masts, as though bidding us a royal farewell from our homeland and a welcome from Britain's sovereign, King George III. I took this all in quietly; it touched me deeply, and I knew that all was well.

After the ships had moved along at full sail for a few hours, we were called below deck to receive our first meal aboard ship. The cooks offered up a light fare of salad, fruit, boiled fish and potatoes. I was so hungry by then that I gobbled it all up in no time. Then, I sat looking around, waiting for someone to go up to the cooks for more. But most of the grown-ups were only half way through their meals. Mother had been watching me. She knew I was looking for a second helping. She nudged my arm, looking toward the serving table, nodding her head slightly. I knew it meant: 'Go for it.' At the counter, the server looked at me and said, "Ah, comin' for more, are yeh?"

"Yes, sir," I replied.

"Here, let me fill your bowl. Eat all the fruit and salad you can get the next few days. Once we are out on the ocean, there won't be much of this kind of food to be had."

"Thank you, sir," I said. "The food is real good."

"Glad you are enjoying it, young fellow. You'll probably dislike some of your future meals of beans, peas and dry bread that will be served up before we reach the colonies. Much depends on how long it takes us to get there and how far we can stretch our food supplies."

By the time we finished eating, it was dusk outside. Mother and I went on deck to enjoy the fresh air and watch the distant dark strip of land disappear beyond the horizon. It was fun to watch, but we also knew we were at sea, for sure. There was no turning back. As we were about to go below deck for our first night's sleep aboard the *Spring*, Papa dropped by. He had been

JHS

busy getting his men settled, and now he could take a few moments to check on us once again.

"Well, I hope your bellies are full. We probably won't eat again until later in the morning."

Mother asked if we would be heading straight for the ocean, leaving the British Isles to our right, along the way.

"Not quite," Father replied. "Right now we are sailing for Portsmouth, on England's southern coast, where we will meet a large contingent of British transports and men of war, in whose company we will continue on to North America. We'll probably have to lay at anchor off Portsmouth for several days until the British Admiral gives the orders to sail before we can proceed. The way I understand it, the ships will be sailing in a prescribed order, forming a close convoy. This improves everyone's safety while at sea. In case of a serious mishap to one ship, others nearby can provide assistance."

While our sergeant was still with us, I asked, "Papa, have you found a drum yet?"

"No, son," he replied. "I haven't forgotten. I'll keep trying."

"Do you think you could borrow a drum, just so I could begin practicing? Doesn't your regimental band have several drums? I saw some of their bandsmen, they are on board with us."

"Good idea, son. I'll look up the bandmaster the next chance I get. Maybe he can help."

With that, he wished us a good night and headed across the deck to the other side of the ship while we clambered down the narrow stairs to the civilian sleeping spaces.

I had a restless night. My hammock kept swinging back and forth as the ship rolled with the waves. While I thought it might rock me to sleep, I was consciously hanging on to the hammock, fearing I might fall out and onto the hard deck. To make things worse, several others in our billeting area snored loudly all night long and kept me awake. When reveille was played, I was so tired and ready to fall asleep, but that chance had been lost. We had to get to the galley early, rather than later in the morning as my father had suggested, because the soldiers on board would be following on our heels. When the soldiers came, that meant get out of their way! As soon as I got the sand out of my eyes, I looked around for my mother. She had jumped out of her bunk as soon as the morning signal was given and had cleaned up in the women's washroom. She was ready to go eat. It didn't take long for me to get ready either; I just skipped washing and joined her on the way to the galley for the morning fare of porridge, bread and milk.

After breakfast, we spent some time on deck, sitting and watching the sailors as they clambered up and down the masts and spars, adjusting ropes and sails as orders were shouted at them by one of the naval officers. It was very damp and foggy, but the water was calm. So far, being on a ship at sea hadn't made my stomach feel woozy, as my father had forewarned before we cast off. I hoped that our journey would continue this way. While we were observing the activity on board, some of the soldiers of the Ditfurth Regiment came up from below and were assigned to assist several of the sailors swabbing the upper deck. The men were a bit timid as they mopped, trying to avoid splashing their uniforms with the grimy water. Salt water, when dried, leaves spots on their clothes, one of the men told me when I observed that his uniform had been badly splashed by one of his buddies who was mopping in back of him. He had caught my attention when I heard his outburst of curses. I didn't know if he was right. My clothes had not suffered any splashing.

Mother had gone below in the meantime. When she returned, she sat on a pile of folded sails and started working on my uniform, as she had said she would. I was thrilled watching her stitch the blue cloth of my uniform jacket. It won't be long now, I thought. I was so engrossed in her work on my uniform that I was just hanging around, doing nothing, just watching. She looked at me, laughed, and said, "You are something else, you didn't even wash up this morning. Shame on you. How can you be a proud drummer marching ahead of all the other soldiers having a dirty face? Instead of standing around, you ought to go below deck and clean up, as you should have done earlier in the day. Go on, and come back with clean hands and face, or I won't sew another stitch!"

I knew she had laughed, but also that she was somewhat upset. I said, "Okay. Mother, I'll do as you say. I'll be right back," and I took off down the steep stairs heading for the men's washroom. When I got there, a grimy sailor was slinging around a mop drenched with dirty water. He seemed to be in a bad mood, for when he spotted me, he said, "What do you want in here? Can't you see I'm trying to clean up this mess? Stay out of here until I'm done and the floor is dry, and if the ship's mate finds your footprints on the deck, I'll be sure to tell him to put you to work down here. Do you understand?"

So, what was I supposed to do? She said to clean up and the grouchy sailor told me to stay out of the washroom. I was confused. I couldn't go back and tell her I did not clean up, she would get real mad at me and probably tell Papa when she saw him next. So, I asked the sailor if I could get a bucket of water to take to the upper deck so I could wash my face and hands. He looked at me with a stern face and shouted, "No, get out of here, now, before I give you a good spanking."

That was it. I said no more. By then, I was afraid of him and I took off.

I felt like crying and sneaked through the ship instead of going back to the top to re-join my mother. To me, walking through the innards of the ship was like an exploratory excursion, a diversion from the setbacks. All I did was look around and watch. At one point, I encountered an assembly of soldiers engaged in prayer. I asked around and found out the regiment's parson was conducting services on board ship, both for the soldiers and in some instances, the families who were accompanying them. As I moped along, I came across a supply room packed with bags of dry goods, where I saw beans, peas, oats, barley and large containers labeled "biscuits." Further along there were more soldiers, some busy cleaning their muskets and others at an inspection of their uniforms. Thinking about what I was seeing, I was impressed that everyone seemed to have a job to do, keeping busy doing something. Back on the upper deck, I watched a detail of soldiers doing calisthenics, and lo and behold, my father was their drill sergeant. When he spotted me, he waved and smiled, but continued with the 'one-two, one-two' cadence his men were following as they jumped up and down in place.

As I continued my way back to my mother, I realized that I still had not washed up.

I've got to do something about it before she tells me again that I have a dirty face, I thought. I'll try the washroom again. The grouchy sailor ought to be out of there by now.

I was determined to find a way to wash up, and I finally did. As I headed straight for the men's washroom, I found it had been cleaned and that no one else was in it. It didn't take but a moment to wrest my shirt off my back and douse myself with several hands full of cool, clear water. But what was that taste? It tasted like salt. Oh, my gosh, that's ocean water, I thought. Another unexpected setback. Everything had gone wrong that day, our first day at sea. But, I did wash my face and hands, and I felt wide awake. That done, I charged up the narrow stairs to the spot where my mother had been sitting, but she was no longer there. Some of the other civilian dependents that had been on deck when I walked away earlier were also no longer around.

What's going on? I thought.

When one of the other children came up from below deck holding a piece of bread, I realized I must have missed lunch and hustled down to the galley, where I found mother and I was able to chisel a few hunks of dry bread from the cook on duty. Luckily, he also gave me a glass of milk that had warmed up by then.

"Where in the world have you been? I got worried when you didn't return as you said you would. What happened? Did you get into trouble?"

"No, Mother, everything is all right. I just got delayed watching the soldiers doing different things. But, I did wash up. Don't I look clean?"

"You certainly do. You must have just done so. Your hair is still wet, and so are your pants. You must have waited to clean up until you were about to join me for lunch? You waited all that time to wash yourself? I can't imagine how sloppy you have become in such a short time. From now on, son, I want you to get to the washroom the minute the reveille signal sounds in the morning, you hear?"

"Yes, Mother. It's just that I was so tired this morning. I hadn't slept a wink before it was time to get up. All because of the moving hammock and the men that were snoring all around me all night."

"I hope you are tired and worn out by the time we turn in. That'll help you sleep."

The next morning, I was one of the first to hit the deck when reveille sounded, and I dashed into the washroom, doing just as Mother had lectured the night before. Breakfast was simple, consisting of crackers, milk and an apple. When Mother and I went up on deck, an early morning shroud of heavy fog surrounded us, which didn't help the movement of our ship. It was edging forward at a snail's pace. A man in the crow's nest called to the captain with steering instructions so he could guide the ship through the dense fog. The lookout was perched high up on one of the tall masts, which allowed him a wider view, so essential for safe sailing. Concurrently, a signal horn sounded periodically to warn nearby sister ships that they may be too close to the *Spring*.

"It's scary, isn't it?" I said to my mother.

"I'd rather see the sun," she replied.

"I don't like to be sitting in the fog not knowing how far away the next ship is. It's like having a bag over our heads with no way to see. At least we're not hearing any horn signals that seem too close," I commented.

"Well," said Mother, "I think the sun will burn the fog off as soon as it rises higher in the sky. That shouldn't take too long. In the meantime, we'll have to remain alert to the sounds around us. I'm sure the captain is doing everything he can to keep moving without hitting another ship. As long as they stay on course, we ought to be all right. The more difficult part for the ships is to maintain their prescribed distances from one another. It is essential that you see what's ahead and around you."

"In the meantime, I'll strain my eyes to see if I can make out anything," I replied.

Within the hour, the fog lifted and the sun shined brightly, just as she had wished for, and a cool breeze filled our sails. While we were sitting around, Mother told me that there was talk of occupying the children's time by holding classes each morning after breakfast, and that the idea may become reality in a day or so.

"Why do they want to start school while we are afloat?" I asked.

"Some of the parents feel the children will be missing out on their schooling if they are allowed to do nothing for days on end. It is not good for the mind."

"And, what do you think?"

"Peter, you know that you have absolutely nothing constructive to do but hang around. I know I will enjoy becoming active in a schooling project even while we are aboard ship. Don't forget, we may be underway for several more weeks or months before we reach the colonies."

"And what will happen to all the sewing you wanted to do to make my uniform?" I asked.

"Now Peter, you know I have been working on it all along. Don't worry, it will be ready by the time you are eligible to wear it," she replied.

The transport moved along nicely for the rest of the day. I sat on a pile of sails staring out at the moving sea and thinking, just thinking, while Mother kept busy working on my uniform. Just before dusk, we joined the others in the messing facility for the evening meal, and soon after, turned in for the night. Life was becoming routine by this time. The days following passed with few changes. The weather held out and onboard activities continued as before among the various groups of travelers. School for the Weinfeld and Meyer children, as well as for me and a few others, began with Mother holding their attention by reading old seafaring stories to them. The children could readily relate their present situations to the yarn of the sailors, except for any experi-

ences with raging seas that swallowed up whole ships and their
crews, as Mother had read to them.

At the second session, little Fritz Meyer asked: "Frau Bauer, do
you think we will run into a storm like the one you read about
yesterday?"

"We do not know these things and must pray to be spared
from such frightful experiences. At any rate, be sure to remember
that you are to stay close to your parents and follow their instructions and those of the ship's captain."

I spoke up. "What if there is a storm and I am on deck, away
from where we are billeted?"

"Peter, in a storm you should not be wandering off to other
parts of the ship on your own. Children should stay near their
parents and other grown-ups. In our case, you should stay near
me. But if you find yourself in the situation you just described, you
should immediately go below deck and make your way back to
your assigned billeting area. This is where your parents, the crew
and others looking for you would expect to find you in an emergency."

Margarite, the Weinfeld girl, asked, "Would our ship turn over
and go down if a big wave hit it?"

"Margarite, these are large ships," Mother replied. "They have
sailed the oceans many times before, and they have been through
many storms and rough seas; you can depend on them to carry us
across the big water safely.

"Remember, they were built by highly skilled shipwrights who
serve the King of Britain, so they must be dependable," she continued. "The stories I have been reading to you speak of times in
the past, when ships were much smaller than they are today. In
those days, sailing across the Atlantic was a dangerous undertak-
ing, but in our time, crossing the ocean has become routine for
sea captains, their crews and their ships.

"Tomorrow, we will do some arithmetic," she went on. "Let's
try to figure out how fast our ship, the *Spring*, is sailing under present weather conditions. That ought to be fun. Knowing that, we
can also calculate how long it will take us to reach North America.
Would you like to do that?"

"Then, we could make a calendar and mark the days remaining before we reach our destination," Margarite answered.

"Yes, but we would have to make allowances for unforeseen weather conditions, like choppy seas or the lack of a driving wind," Mother responded. She then told the children that Parson Johann Hofmeister of the Ditfurth Regiment would join them for the next session to explain the mathematical calculations.

Regrettably, the arithmetic class had to be canceled when the  Parson was summoned to bury a sailor at sea who had fallen from the crow's nest the past night. The young man had lost his footing climbing up the rope ladder to relieve his shipmate. His steep fall to the deck below had killed him instantly. The captain ordered the burial to be held while the children were attending school. Mother explained to the children that the Parson had other commitments that morning, but that he was looking forward to spending some time with them soon.

Parson Hofmeister greeted the assembled children three days later. At that time, the sea was much rougher than on prior days and blowing salt spray was wetting down everything on the upper deck and above. Under the circumstances, the compartment below deck, in which the children had gathered, made for a dry and cozy environment. Standing in front of the room, explaining the method of calculating the ship's speed, the Parson suddenly lost his balance due to the ship's rolling motion. The children screamed as he fell, but he was back on his feet quickly, explaining that the fall had been his own fault due to his failure to consider the circumstances of the day; namely, the rough sea and the unusual rocking of the ship. His reassuring words were insufficient, however. The motion of the ship was affecting the equilibrium of several children. Little Fritz turned pale, complaining of not feeling well. Mother, who was assisting the parson, agreed the boy should be dismissed to the care of his parents. She then walked young Fritz to the section where the boy's family was staying and dropped him off. Mrs. Meyer, who was sitting on her bunk reading, thanked Mother for bringing him to her, offering to read to Fritz for the duration of his absence from class.

The other children, though somewhat shaky themselves, were enjoying the arithmetic lesson the parson was teaching. On completion, he prayed with the students for a safe journey across the rough waters in the days ahead. Then, Mother made sure all of the children returned to their assigned compartments and families.

For several more days, the ships traveled westward between France and Britain, eventually changing course to a northwesterly direction, and heading straight for Portsmouth. During those intervening days, the ship's routine hardly changed. Mother was busy sewing most of the time, and I attended classes and did my homework. We hardly ever saw my father, who was our sponsor. He and the soldiers stayed busy from morning to night with various military duties and assignments. To top it off, the captain delegated certain ship housekeeping chores to Colonel Ditfurth and the men in his regiment. There was hardly a moment the soldiers had to themselves or their families. When the sun went down, the men turned in for the night. Trying to read or play cards by candlelight below deck was little fun, especially when the seas were rough, and pushed and rocked the ship in every direction. That was usually the time to "hit the sack" and forget one's plight.

Several more days elapsed before the lookout shouted, "Land Ho!" Those on the upper deck rushed to the starboard side to see for themselves, straining their eyes for a personal peek at the thin shadow of land on the distant horizon.

"That must be Portsmouth," someone uttered. A few hours later, after changing direction, it was confirmed that the ship's formation was heading for Portsmouth to meet up with the British, who had been assembling there for several days, waiting for the first contingent of Hessians to arrive. As the ships drew closer to land, many ships at anchor could be sighted. Among them were large and small transports, and a number of sizable men of war with their escorts.

"Mother," I said, "Just look at all these ships; they must be waiting for us. See the big ones with all their cannons? They call them 'men of war' because they can stand alone and protect themselves in a fight. I guess they will be coming along to protect us on our way across the ocean. Can you imagine just how much cargo those real big transports can haul away? Several have three or more decks, and then the holds below. They must be able to carry a lot of soldiers, as well as their equipment. I wonder how many ships there are in total."

Mother replied, "What a sight. I have never seen this many ships in one place in all my life. There must be at least 50 or more that I can count from here, and there are more behind that spit of land to our left. Maybe it's the big island we have to pass on our way into the harbor. Yes, I can see many more masts sticking out in the distance."

"Take a good look at the warships," I pointed out. "They all have a long string of guns on the upper deck. See those square holes along the top? There's a gun in each one of them. I wouldn't want to get too close to them if I were an enemy. Their heavy cannon balls could knock your sails down in no time."

On approaching the first ship at anchor, the captain ordered his crew to strike the sails and drop anchor, keeping a safe distance from the ship ahead.

I continued, "Look, that's a transport that has British soldiers on it. See their red jackets? There are a lot of them on the upper deck. I imagine they are looking at us wondering who we are and what we are like."

"You are right, Peter," Mother replied. "They must have anchored a day or two before we arrived. They couldn't afford to keep their soldiers aboard ship for any length of time, just hanging around and doing nothing. The soldiers are getting paid, and the King can expect something in return. So as not to waste time, the British must be aiming for an early departure, now that we are here."

While the *Spring* was maneuvering into position, the ships following her began dropping sails and lowering their anchors.

At the end of the 11-day trip, my father was able to check on us once again. He greeted Mother with a hug and put his hand on my head in a gesture of recognition.

"Well, it's been days since I last saw the two of you," he said. "I have been with the troops, training and preparing them for the long journey ahead. I hope the two of you feel at home aboard ship by now. We'll have to be satisfied living in close quarters like this for many weeks to come. I never realized crossing the ocean could take up to three months, depending on the weather we encounter, but that's what they tell me."

Mother replied, "Well, Karl, I suppose we can't complain. After all, we chose to accept the regiment's invitation to accompany you on the expedition. So far, we have been doing all right. My problem is that I feel so hemmed in with no way to get off. I do miss the countryside back home. I'd love to walk the fields. And, of course, our young Peter is completely bored. He sits watching me trying to sew his uniform, but with the constant rocking motion of the ship, that is very difficult to do. And that becomes frustrating to both of us."

"I hope the two of you can adjust to your new situation. Try to put the farm and the fields out of your mind, Anna. And you, Peter, start doing something worthwhile instead of just watching your Mother sew. A boy can do many things, starting with shining your shoes. Maybe you could beat the dust out of your clothes. Your duds must be full of dust by now, lying around like you have been. You know, we soldiers have to do this periodically. Some of us even have our own cat-of-nine-tails for that purpose. I'll let you have mine if you want to use it. Just try to adapt. Keep in mind, there is land on the other side of the ocean that we will get to in due course. Your goal should be to keep busy until we get there. Life will be much better once we reach the colonies. Unfortunately, we can't disembark here at Portsmouth; that would have given you a chance to stretch your legs. Nonetheless, I imagine the King's men are concerned that some of us might not return to our ships if we were allowed to go on land."

"Papa," I asked, "How many ships are out there? Do you know?"

"We have been told we would be sailing in the company of 80 or more ships of all types and sizes. Looking at all the masts around us, that figure makes a lot of sense. It sounds realistic.

Don't forget, we joined them with 20 ships ourselves. We only paid attention to the larger transports that sailed with us, although many others came along. The smaller ones don't carry wagons and horses, but they are packed with our tents and other equipment we will need as soon as we set foot on land again."

"Anna," Papa continued, "If I'm correct, you and some of the ladies will be asked to start making some medical supplies, like bandages and the like. The medical officer wants his chest of supplies to be well stocked and ready for any situation. We were beginning to think, 'What if some of the dissident colonists resist our presence?' Actually, any adverse action on their part may be far fetched, but one needs to be prepared for the unexpected. The British have even started calling the dissidents 'rebels' for their refusal to pay the taxes their King has levied, as is done with us by the Landgrave. We wouldn't do that. I don't know what these colonists are thinking. Why should they be exempt from their sovereign's law?"

"Karl, do you think you will actually have to fight these people?" Mother asked.

"I hope not. But we are soldiers. If we have to, we will confront them and put them down in the name of the King. We would have no other choice," he said.

"Father, what is expected of you?" I inquired.

"Well, son, when ordered, soldiers do battle with anyone who opposes them. If the King directs us to disperse demonstrators or any armed opposition, we will do so by doing whatever it takes for us to prevail," he replied.

"What if there are a lot of them and they won't disperse?"

"In such case we will use force."

"Like what?" I inquired.

"Peter, when and if ordered, we would use force at a level needed to succeed. In a dire case, we would use our muskets without hesitation."

"Would you kill them if they stood up to you?"

"Though hard to do, Peter, we would match their resistance at a superior level to put them down, even if it meant that some would perish in the process," Papa noted.

I went silent after this exchange. The answers I received were too difficult and complex for me to comprehend. Although I knew the British and Hessians would confront the dissidents in an effort to alter their present negative attitudes toward the King, I had not given much thought to the realities of the situation and that casualties, even death, could result among the sparring parties. So I just sat, withdrawn and in deep thought, fearful of what may lay ahead.

Papa then said, "And here's the good news, Peter. Listen up, I spoke with Captain Max Feller, our regimental bandmaster."

"You did? What did he say?" I asked, anticipating Papa's response.

"When the convoy is underway a few days after leaving Portsmouth, the band will begin practicing on deck every few days, weather permitting. Their music will entertain the troops at the same time. On days when there is no practice, Captain Feller will devote some of his time to instructing his drummers, including you, Master Peter. Because of the deep and loud resounding drum beats, you fellows will probably have to practice below deck, maybe in one of the lower cargo holds. The other members of the band will be able to show off their skills on deck. However, they too, will be getting into some basic stuff below deck to refresh and sharpen their individual skills. You will just have to be satisfied with what the bandmaster is willing to do for you ahead of your official acceptance and designation as drummer boy."

"Oh, Papa, I am so excited. Thank you so much. I promise to do good, and I'm sorry if I thought you had forgotten about me and the drum. I love you, Papa."

"Well, Peter," he replied, "There is no chance to repair your drum aboard ship as we had hoped. The wagon master just can't come up with the right kind of wood to do the job. Maybe we can pick up on that idea again after we land in the colonies. Right now, you'll at least have a chance to learn the basics of drumming and begin practicing on someone else's drum; that ought to satisfy your most urgent wishes. Good luck. I will be keeping an eye on you as you get deeper into your program with Captain Feller."

Mother then commented. "I am happy for you, Peter, but you must be well kempt at all times, face and hands washed. And remember, you will be practicing under the watchful eye of one of the Landgrave's favorite officers. Captain Feller deserves the greatest respect. He is one of the senior officers in your father's regiment."

"Sure, I'll be the cleanest and best-dressed drummer you have ever seen, even without a uniform."

"I am glad, and your uniform is coming along well. By the time your birthday comes around, you'll probably know all about drumming, and you'll have your uniform by then, too," she replied.

After Papa returned to his troop compartment, Mama and I spent time observing the activity aboard the ship. It was exciting to watch all that was going on. Several crews from nearby ships were rowing to the docks to pick up barrels of fresh water, and our own captain left to meet the British Admiral aboard his flagship anchored in the bay. They took one of the sailors ashore to receive expert medical attention. Apparently, he was too ill for the ship's doctor to treat him aboard ship. Some time later, the skiff returned without him. If they don't bring him back by the time we get underway, he'll have to stay behind, I thought. In that case, they would probably reassign him to some ship with a later sailing date.

"There's a lot going on out there, isn't there?"

"Oh, yes," Mother said. "There are still a lot of preparations to be made before the tall ships can venture out the channel to the open sea. The British admiral has to make sure all the captains are familiar with his sailing plan. I imagine it must be tricky, sailing in a convoy formation. All movements must be performed with precision to avoid collisions or other mishaps, especially in rough seas and at night. I imagine the admiral has a lot to talk about – the signals he will be giving en route, and the various maneuvers he will be ordering under different circumstances. After the briefings, the captains are expected to follow his guidance when sailing their ships. There are a multitude of captains' skiffs out there. They must be carrying the top officers from every ship to a meeting with the admiral. Peter, as I observe all of this, I feel much more secure than I was when we left home. It is good to know that the British admiral has everything under control."

"All those little boats in the water look like bees buzzing around, going every which way. I guess the harbor is to us what a beehive is to them," I noted.

"That is a good comparison," Mother replied. "I'm glad you are so observant and reason out situations as you just did. That is what Papa and I meant when we said that you ought to be more active, keeping busy for the duration of the trip. Watching, observing and trying to figure things out is part of it. Keep it up and you will not be bored. Actually, you will be seeing and learning things none of your friends back home could ever imagine. Just think about it, you – young Master Bauer – crossing the ocean on a great big ship in the company of close to 100 others like it. Who could envision such a sight? Our townsfolk have never seen a single ship of the size we are on, never mind a gathering of ships as we are seeing here right now."

For me, there was little to do for the next few days while the ships were taking on supplies for the long journey. I wandered about the ship impatiently, trying to pass the time, anxiously waiting for the sailing orders. I was wrapped up in thought, anticipating the drummer training Papa had described. I moved about the main deck looking at this and that, but nothing impressed me enough to make me stop thinking. Although I seemed to be looking at the ships at anchor, I was actually staring into the distance, maybe seeing myself marching about the deck beating a drum and trying to keep up with my own cadence. Sometimes, I was watching the gulls hanging in the sky above, just riding the wind without moving their wings. I wondered why people couldn't do that. It would be fun if we could. During these times, the world and time just seemed to pass while my mind was somewhere else.

CHAPTER 11

Off to America

Several more days passed until the admiral's ship fired a cannon at daybreak on May 5. The loud discharge broke the still of morning, waking sailors, soldiers and the accompanying civilians aboard the ships in the harbor. Everyone quickly left their hammocks and bunks, rushing to take up their stations. The cannon blast gave notice to the ships' captains to weigh their anchors and sail through the passage to the open water. The many vessels were buzzing with activity, as sailors hustled about raising anchors and setting sails to orders barked by their captains and ship's officers. Extra hands were always welcome to carry out these maneuvers with precision, and the captains availed themselves of the extra muscle the soldiers aboard their ships could provide.

Mother and I grabbed a piece of dry bread as we ran for the upper deck, getting in the way of rushing crewmembers. Neither of us wanted to miss the departure. It would be a once-in-a-lifetime experience, seeing all these ships leaving their berths and anchorage's at short intervals.

Mother touched my arm and said, "Look, Peter, isn't this magnificent?"

"You bet. Do you see that real big one with the very tall masts leading the parade? She's a giant among all the others, and the first to make her way out to sea. I wonder if this ship is of any special significance, considering her size and all."

Just then, Papa came along to greet us on this historic day, when the ships loaded with British and Hessian soldiers were finally setting sail for the British colonies in North America. "How do you like that? Just look at all these ships, and the thousands of sails. This will be going on for the rest of the day. Isn't it breathtaking?"

"Papa, what is that towering tall ship that's leading the way?" I asked. "It is gigantic, much bigger than several of our transports put together."

"Oh, that is the H.M.S. Victory, Admiral Keppel's flagship – the King's largest man of war. Built in 1765, it has a displacement of some 2,100 tons and is about 180 feet long. The masts are exceptionally tall. To support their height and heavy sails, the main mast has a diameter of close to 40 inches and rises well over 100 feet above the water. And the yards, or cross arms as we landlubbers call them, are also close to 100 feet long".

"It looks like the H.M.S. Victory has three decks," I observed.

"Well, that's what you can see, the decks above the waterline. There are several holds below them," Papa added. "Notice the gun ports. You can see them on the three decks, positioned along the entire length of the ship. It looks like there are 44 on each side, that would give you a total of 88 guns altogether. That makes the H.M.S. Victory a virtually invincible floating fort."

"Papa, from where does the admiral give instructions to his people?"

"He'll probably stay near the helm, that is near the steering section. From there, he can see what's going on topside and also, what the other ships are doing."

Mother then asked: "Karl, how long can the Victory stay at sea without having to take on fresh supplies?"

"They tell us she can carry supplies for six months, Anna. She has all the facilities needed to support any venture for that duration, including a large sick bay and various shops essential to keep the ship and equipment in good repair."

His statement prompted me to ask, "You said they have a large sick bay. Why? Do the sailors get seasick?"

"The sailors are pretty seasoned and can handle the constant rocking of the ship, but what gets some of them down is scurvy if they are at sea for months on end – especially if their diets lack citrus fruits. To prevent or forestall scurvy, people need to eat oranges and lemons, even drink lime juice. These commodities become increasingly scarce the longer their ship is at sea. Scurvy can result in serious weakness, loss of hair and, what's truly noticeable, the loss of teeth."

"Papa," I asked, "Do you think the sailor who spoke with me, you know the one who looked real ugly and had hardly a tooth in his mouth, might have suffered from scurvy at some time?"

"Son, I venture he may well be the victim of scurvy, especially if he has been a mariner with many prolonged sailings to his credit."

While we were talking, several other ships passed, some with soldiers standing about the decks waving. I waved back with enthusiasm. From their red tunics, one could tell they were British. The many ships heading out to sea made an impressive sight. Mother heard me say aloud to nobody in particular, "That's a real parade of sail." She smiled.

Papa then said, "Our ship will be getting in line pretty quickly now. I had better get back to my station before I am called. Enjoy the rest of the day. I'll see you sometime in the morning." With that, he hugged Mother and gave me a friendly tap on the shoulder.

Walking away, he added, "H.M.S. Victory will be escorting the convoy to the open ocean. Once we are a safe distance from the mainland, Admiral Keppel will return to Portsmouth and leave the escort duties to several other man of war ships that are making their way out of the harbor at this time."

"Bye, Papa!" I yelled.

Mother then said, "Peter, I am going below. I want to check on how far along I am with sewing your uniform so I can get started again once the excitement is over. Then, we can organize our time better. Remain on deck if you wish, but stay out of trouble."

"I will," I replied as I began walking about the deck, listening as the captain gave orders to one of the ship's officers who prompted a group of sailors to unfurl more sail, enabling the *Spring* to pick up speed and fall in line with the other ships as they headed toward the British Channel, one by one. It took hours for the entire fleet to clear Portsmouth harbor and the nearby waters. Later in the afternoon, I looked about in amazement when I noted the many ships that had lined up in a convoy formation, all heading west while keeping safe distances from one another. By then, stronger winds were prevalent and the ships were beginning to move along at an accelerated pace.

In all the excitement, I had missed lunch and I was getting tired. I decided to chance the galley to see if the cook might give me something to eat. I left the upper deck and headed for the galley, abandoning the thrill of watching the fleet. I was lucky; the cook was there, busy stirring a cauldron of steaming hot vegetable soup that would be served to all hands a bit later.

"Sir, might I have a piece of bread? I have been on deck watching the fleet all day as the ships were leaving the harbor and missed lunch. Now I am starved. I'll die if I have to wait for the evening meal."

"This must have been very exciting for you, seeing all these ships," the cook replied, "and I can understand that you missed your noon meal. Of course, with an empty belly you are dragging your body around. That's an effort, isn't it?" he continued. "Well, young man, how would you like a taste of the soup I am making. You can let me know what you think of it."

"Wow, I'd like that very much. I'll tell you what it's like, sir. I won't need any bread if I eat the soup."

"Well, young fellow, how about if I give you a piece of hard leftover bread along with your soup? You can dunk it in the broth to soften it up, all right?"

"Sir, that's a real meal. I won't be able to eat supper later on."

With that, the cook handed me a piece of hard bread and then scooped a large ladle of soup into a messing tin. My eyes popped when I saw what the cook was doing. I was speechless when I was handed the food, and I looked at the cook with a big approving grin of gratitude.

The cook then said: "Go, find a place to sit and eat while it's hot."

I gobbled down the hot soup and the bread in no time. My demeanor showed I was enjoying every bit of it. I thanked the cook when I had finished and told him it had been the best soup I had ever tasted. He smiled and said, "Run along now. I have more to do before the mealtime signal."

When my belly was full again, I clambered back to the upper deck, just to see how things were progressing. In my mind, I was envisioning myself as captain of the ship. Of course, I had to assure myself that everything was under control. When I reached the open deck, I positioned myself so I could observe what was happening on deck, while at the same time watching the progress of the ships in front and off both sides of my ship, the *Spring*. I could tell that my facial expressions changed from time to time as my mind was processing the various observations I was making. If anyone was watching, an occasional smile on my part would have given away my satisfaction with some of the things I was observing. But occasionally, there were also some stern expressions during which my facial muscles tightened, signs that some things were not going as well as they should, in my opinion. The ever-present saltwater spray added realism to my role-playing as captain of the ship.

A sudden clanging of the ship's bell startled me out of my dream world. I stood silently for a moment, wondering where I might be, and why someone would be ringing the bell without my orders. But I quickly recovered when I realized it was the bell announcing chow time that I had heard. I went below to locate my mother. She was talking with Johann Hofmeister, the regiment's chaplain.

When she saw me, she said: "Here he comes. I am sure he will not be enthused about school starting up again in a few days."

"We'll make it interesting for the children," the parson said. "They will learn about the sea, the clouds and the weather. I am sure we will be able to hold their interest."

I had overheard the parson's remarks, and I added a comment of my own. "Actually, sir, what we will be learning is of interest to me. I was just playing sea captain on the upper deck and wondered about such things as choppy seas and stormy weather, and what effect they might have on sailing the ship."

"Well, Master Peter, you will be hearing and experiencing lots about weather and the sea around us in the coming days and weeks," he answered.

"You will actually be learning much through personal experiences as we proceed along the path that has been placed before us. This is a very unique journey we are allowed to undertake, and it may provide us all with some great opportunities to learn about the environment in which we live and our places and roles in it," he continued.

What the parson was saying was a bit too much for me. I didn't quite understand what he was trying to tell me, so I replied with a weak, "Yes, sir."

He then said, "You say you were playing sea captain. Tell me, Master Peter, do you think you would like to command a ship and sail the high seas when you grow up?"

"No, sir," I replied, "I'd like to become a drummer. I think that would be the neatest thing, having all the soldiers march to my drumbeat."

"But you can't be a drummer boy all your life. What would you like to do when you get older?"

"Oh, I'll be a soldier, just like my father. I like his sharp uniform, and he takes care of us and is always looking out for our well-being. I love him. He's the best."

"And what about your mother?" the parson asked. "She takes care of you all the time, and even more so when your father is away."

"Oh yes, she looks after me and makes sure I eat well and stay out of trouble. I do love her very much. She's good to me, but I'll love her even more when she finishes my uniform one of these days."

The parson looked at Mother, smiling, and then took leave, saying: "Well, I will now partake of the cook's latest creation. They say he's making vegetable soup. I'll be seeing you in school in a few days, Master Peter. Good night to both of you."

Soon after he left, Mother and I headed for the galley to savor the hot vegetable soup I had sampled earlier. It still tasted good. When my mother tried it, all I could hear was "Umm," quiet sounds of approval. She was enjoying it, just as I had when I first tasted the soup. To be sure, I went for a second helping and ate until I was bloated. When we finished, we headed to our assigned sleeping spaces to relax. It had been a long and exciting day for everyone and soon we were all sound asleep.

I met my mother at the galley in the morning. We both agreed we had a good night's sleep and were now hungry enough to eat a horse. While we were enjoying some hot porridge, Papa joined us for a cup of early morning tea.

"We are on our way," he said, " We are a part of what we call the First Division that is heading for the North American colonies. Another convoy of our size will be following in a few weeks. By the time they get there, I am sure we will have settled in pretty well. Maybe things will be under control by then, so we can think of heading back home. That would be nice, wouldn't it?"

"If that is indeed the case, Karl. We will all have made a long vacation trip we otherwise would never have been able to undertake. But, I think you fellows will have your hands full, trying to make orderly and obedient people out of the rebels over there," Mother said. "Let's pray for our safety and God's grace as we cross the big water, and for the duration of our stay on the American continent, no matter how long the Landgrave wants you to be there."

"You are right," Papa replied. "General Leopold Philip von Heister is in charge of our First Division. They couldn't have picked a better man. He's truly from the elite in many respects. Not only has he been a soldier for most of his life, he is as alert and clever as a fox, and as shrewd as can be. Nothing gets past him that isn't perfect. We can be thankful he's our top general. He'll do whatever has to be done to make this a successful campaign so he can return home to glory before he retires."

I then asked, "Is he the highest officer?"

"No, Peter," Papa replied. "For now, General von Heister is the highest ranking Hessian general accompanying the Landgrave's troops to the continent. Although he is in charge of the Hessian units, in the end, he has to answer to the British commander who is responsible to the King."

"Anyway," he continued, "soon we'll be completely surrounded by the ocean. There will be no turning back, and communications between the ships will be by signals, flags and cannon shots. That means we'll be on our own from here on. So be especially alert and try not to get hurt when you wander among all the ropes and sails stacked on the decks. And stay out of the sailors' way. They have tough and hard jobs to perform, sometimes very dangerous. Just keep these things in mind as you while away your days at sea."

"Yes, Papa, I understand," I replied.

During the next few days, the ships sailed their prescribed courses without any unforeseen delays or mishaps. Sunny days allowed the dependent family members to spend time on deck to enjoy the sun's rays and the sea mist as the ships' bows cut through the calm waters. For the children, it was a time of fun and laughter as they played hide-and-go-seek among the piles of sails and ropes and other supplies that had been stacked around the upper deck. But that lasted only until one of the ship's mates yelled at them in a deep, throaty pirate-like voice to go elsewhere lest they be thrown in the brig. Not wanting word of the scolding to reach my father, I got away as fast as I could. Being criticized by my father, the sergeant among a detail of Hessian soldiers, could have turned out to be more embarrassing than being incarcerated in the ship's brig. My friends also found other ways to keep busy. A few of them were soon immersed in a game of jacks, while some of the others rolled out a set of agates. However, to their disappointment, the ship's movements kept the glass balls rolling. This prevented a serious game from getting started.

The young ones, including myself, always welcomed mealtimes and beat the sailors and soldiers to the front of the line to be sure we'd get our share before the food was completely doled out by the cooks.

It was during one of these mess calls that I mentioned that it seemed there were more people in the food line now than there had been when we first sailed to Britain from Bremerlehe. Mother responded by telling me that an additional contingent of Hessian soldiers had joined us just before we sailed from Portsmouth. This resulted in more cramped quarters for the troops and a need for stricter rationing of food.

The conditions she described had not been too noticeable at first; everyone was usually very tired by nightfall and fell asleep quickly. Now that everyone was somewhat settled, the changed conditions became more noticeable, in particular, the odor of the additional sweating bodies and the upsetting smell of sea sickness that almost became unbearable below deck.

To get our minds off the unpleasant conditions, Johann Hofmeister, the regimental chaplain, in consultation with my mother and the other women, agreed to start up schooling for the children. They felt that classes would provide some positive diversions from the discomforts we were experiencing, which wasn't very much other than the negative aspects everyone had noticed. Our new environment and the endless sea of which we all were now a part were subjects we would otherwise not hear much about because of our normally close relationship to the land and the farms from whence most of us had come. Such classes were to help explain our changed living conditions at sea and the differences in our way of life under these circumstances.

CHAPTER 12

The High Sea

Our ships sailed for days on end, making their way through calm as well as rough seas. Soon, life among the crews and their passengers became a matter of routine. For the most part, shipboard activities were carried out in an orderly fashion. Troops, dependents and sailors headed for the galley at designated times to receive their meals three times each day. Time was set aside to clean up and sweep the crew's quarters and other frequented areas on a regular schedule. Weather permitting, bed clothing was brought to the upper deck to be aired out at least once each week.

The soldiers were kept busy. Some could be seen drilling and marching in open areas of the deck or in one of the holds. Occasionally, detachments of soldiers were issued their muskets for cleaning and oiling before returning them to Sergeant Weinfeld, the armorer, who stored the weapons in a secure and safe place under lock and key, ready to be issued when ordered. Twice a week, the band was busy practicing or cleaning their instruments, mostly above deck. As needed, soldiers were detailed to assist the ship's crew whenever they had a need for additional manpower.

On most weekdays, the children received some type of schooling. This occupied the chaplain, as well as my mother, Bertha Meyer, the supply sergeant's wife, and Lotte Weinfeld, the armorer's spouse. Besides tutoring, the women assisted Chaplain Hofmeister in planning and participating actively in the instructional sessions that kept all of us busy.

Mother worked on my uniform whenever she could, but she

took her time. She knew the uniform could be finished up quickly if needed. However, she didn't want to complete the job too soon, expecting I would badger her and Papa for a drum, just so I could wear the uniform even before being formally signed on as a drummer boy. I was keeping a keen eye on my mother and her progress with the uniform. Even though I didn't say much, I was always snooping around to see what she was doing whenever she had a needle and thread in her hands. Understandably, my greatest concern was my uniform. I needed it. It was important to me that I get it soon. I didn't give much thought to Mother's use of needle and thread for other jobs she had, such as sewing torn shirts and patching uniforms for some of the military aboard ship. Mending socks was included in her assignment of maintaining and caring for the uniform and clothing allowances of several Ditfurth personnel.

Papa checked on us, his dependents, as often as his duties would allow, making sure we were well taken care of. He, too, would sneak an occasional peek to keep abreast of the progress on my uniform, knowing I would bring up that subject if I ever caught him alone. He knew of my great enthusiasm, and combining that with my childhood impatience, wanted to be sure he could provide some authoritative answers to any questions I might throw at him regarding the status of my uniform. As a father, he wished the project could be expedited and the uniform presented to me to make me happy, but also to forego my frustrations about the lack of progress. As a husband, he felt Mother was right. There was actually no need to rush more than necessary, simply because there was no urgent need for the uniform until I would be old enough to be signed on. And, as a regimental sergeant, he didn't have the time to hunt for a drum, at least not as long as we were aboard ship. I guess there just weren't any extras around. After landing in the colonies, that issue could demand more of father's attention – after he and the troops calmed down the colonists, which Papa anticipated could require everyone's undivided attention for a period of time.

During the second week of May, sightings of flying fish and porpoises captured the attention of everyone aboard *Spring*, and undoubtedly the soldiers and dependents being carried on the other ships in the convoy. I spent much of my time on deck watching the sea creatures frolic, with the porpoises often coming so close to the ship they made me think they were going to smash into the side of the hull. That could get real dangerous, I thought, letting out excited screams on many such occasions. Nearby crew members watched and laughed at my excited behavior. The first time I spotted a flying fish, I was flabbergasted, for I had never before seen anything like it. Who had ever heard of such a thing as flying fish? Wanting to share my latest discovery, I quickly located my mother.

"Mother, guess what's out there. Fish flying through the air like birds."

Mother had not seen such odd creatures before either, and she figured I was trying to put one over on her. "Come on, Peter, be careful to whom you tell that story. No one will believe you."

"Believe me, there are flying fish out there; they are flying low over the water. Come on and see for yourself. They just come jumping out of the water, then they spread their wings and take off flying until they hit the water again and disappear."

"Peter, Peter, wait 'til I tell your father that you are spreading fish stories."

"Please, come with me; I'll show you."

"All right, I'll let you trick me. But remember, if you are fibbing I will get real mad at you. Let's go."

When we reached the deck, I quickly skipped over to the side of the ship looking to spot the magical fish. "There – look right there. See them? There are lots of them. They are jumping out of the water, buzzing around and diving back into the water. They have wings, too. Do you see them?"

"Why Peter, this is a miracle. I did not believe you until I saw it with my own eyes. You are right. I am sorry to have questioned you. I should have known better. After all, the Parson Hofmeister tells us all the time that we should have faith in one another and the truths we are told. That means we should trust each other and refrain from questioning everything, lest we run the risk of insulting someone. On the other hand, we must insure we are not being taken advantage of by those who would spread rumors or lies."

"That's all right, I couldn't believe my own eyes at first when I saw fish with wings. Who ever heard of such a thing? And then

they were flying about. This is truly something I will never forget. My friends back home would never believe us if we told them what we are seeing right now."

I continued, "The sailors told me to be on the lookout for porpoises. They described them as being real big, looking like small whales. But then, the flying fish popped up out of nowhere. That was real exciting. And the porpoises are now frolicking about in the water. They are fun to watch. But even so, I'm always afraid they might ram into the side of the ship and make it sink."

"Well, Peter, I wouldn't worry about that. This ship has sailed the ocean many times before and nothing of that sort ever happened. Anyway, for now, I am returning to the lower deck. If you make any more unusual sightings, come and get me. I'd like to see these things, too. If you remain on deck, just be careful and stay out of trouble, please. I'll see you later at mealtime."

With that, Mother went below. I stayed on deck, with my eyes glued to the water, hoping to spot a school of porpoises and more of the small flying fish that seemed to be out there in large numbers.

The weather had been holding out very well, even though the convoy hit some rough spots from time to time – in particular – when the winds picked up, causing the ship to rock sufficiently to make walking the decks uneasy, if not treacherous. I lost my balance every now and then, and fell to the deck, often cursing to myself in a subdued voice. I wouldn't dare announce my misgivings too loudly, not wanting to fall into disfavor with my father. After all, it was he who was going to get the drum I needed for my upcoming job as drummer boy. Besides, serving in the same regiment in which my father was a respected sergeant required me to maintain an unblemished record of good behavior.

As usual, our family met in the galley area at mealtime for a little chitchat.

"Well, I imagine you have had some exciting moments watching the porpoises and flying fish," were the first words Papa said when he joined us that evening.

"And, you have been bounced around a bit also, with the ship rocking every which way in the rough water. But, we'll all get used to it once we develop our 'sea legs' and learn to keep our balance like the sailors do."

"Well, Papa, I fell several times these last few days and got a few bruises along the way."

"Did you get hurt? Anything serious?"

"No, I'm fine. I just get mad at falling for no reason."

"Anna, what about you? I imagine you are smart enough to stay off your feet when the ship rocks too much, heh?"

"Karl, you are so right. At such times, I sit somewhere and stay put while sewing or reading. When things calm down, I move around doing some of my assigned chores. All in all, I think we have both been doing well," she concluded.

"Oh, before I forget," he continued, "I wanted you to know that Colonel von Ditfurth called a meeting of his officers today after a discussion he had with the ship's captain. The colonel alerted everyone to be prepared for the possibility of encountering rough seas as we get farther out into the ocean. The captain had spoken from prior experience, passing on information on some of the situations he had encountered on earlier sailings in the same waters. Apparently, it could get real rough if we sail into one of those fierce storms he spoke about. So, we have to give it special attention. I'll let the two of you know immediately if special precautions become necessary. In the meantime, continue enjoying the voyage. Oh yes, Peter, I understand you young'ns are doing real well in studying celestial navigation. The chaplain tells us the young people are interested in the subject, which makes things easier for him. He didn't realize he had such a receptive group among the children on board. Keep up the good work, Peter. There is an awful lot you can learn from Chaplain Hofmeister. He is a good teacher in many ways."

Soon after, Papa bid us a good night as he headed for the troop compartment. Both Mother and I took separate ways to our bunks. I fell into deep sleep and dreamt of the past day's excitement.

CHAPTER 13

Point of No Return

May 21 was exactly the kind of day that Colonel von Ditfurth had been forewarned about by the ship's captain. Rough seas prevailed from the moment the ship's contingent was rousted from their hammocks. Upon being alerted, the soldiers and dependents dressed hurriedly, some foregoing their morning ablutions. For some, it was not a good time to eat. Stomachs were woozy from the ever-rolling seas, and the landlubbers wanted to master their fate with dignity by not baring their weaknesses before the seasoned sailors, who had been posted near every exit and ladder to provide assistance if needed.

During this stressful time, my father made his way through the lower deck to reach us one deck above, and give us the latest update on the weather and any precautionary advice he had received.

In the meantime, the waves had become mountainous, breaking over the deck, tearing sails and tossing anything not tied down into the raging sea. Every now and then, a gusher of angry water spilled down ladders and stairs, filling the compartments ankle-high with foamy sea water. People were being tossed around, falling and screaming as they bounced about among bunks and hammocks. The ship was rocking out of control in no set pattern, with raging waves dictating its movements. To the passengers praying for help and mercy, it seemed the ship was without rudder, and the ship's crew was helpless under these conditions. Thunder and lightning added to nature's fearsome display.

Finally, I spotted Papa as he came in our direction, holding onto whatever was there that would allow him to steady his walk.

"Papa, please help us," I said. "How long will this last? We are both sick to our stomachs. We couldn't eat this morning, and if we had, we wouldn't be able to keep anything down. Where is Chaplain Hofmeister? Is he praying for us? Will God hear him?"

"The best we can do for now is pray for God's mercy and maintain a positive attitude," he replied. "We know the storm cannot last forever. So we have to keep faith and believe that we will survive nature's punishing blows. Remember, we are all being bounced around. Not just the *Spring*, but all the ships in our convoy. Can you imagine the many prayers that are being offered? There are so many, God is sure to hear them. Have you seen your Mother?"

"Yes, Papa, she's over there holding on to her bunk for dear life. But, I can tell, Mom is real strong. The rocking and tossing about of the ship can't pry her hands apart. Look, over there, can you see her?"

"All right, Peter. Be sure you stay below deck and stay close to your mother during this dangerous storm. Do as she says. She knows what's best. I'll stop by to see her for a moment. Then I have to get back to my own compartment. Quite a few of my soldiers are seasick, too. That's not good."

I watched as he wound his way through the sleep area to talk with Mother, before leaving to re-join his men.

The storm lasted a full week without any let-up. At night, people were thrown from their bunks and hammocks, screaming in fear. Crackling lightning strikes lit up the sky for short moments

during the night.

I could hear a sailor on deck yelling: "Look out, there's a transport bouncing in the water alongside ours. Pray to God that he will not plow into us."

People below deck were huddling in corners whimpering and praying for their lives. Phrases like "Hell on earth," and "God has forsaken us," soldiers uttered as I was trying to hang on and maintain my footing. I couldn't suppress a tear as I sought repeatedly to encourage myself, as my parents told me to do. I blew my nose and wiped my face quickly, not wanting to appear afraid, even though deep down, I felt abandoned and lost, like so many others.

During this time of helplessness, all activity on board became disorganized and much of the daily routine fell by the wayside. Still, in their desperation, the crew and the passengers had one thing in common – all prayed for their salvation.

For the sailors, there was much to do whenever circumstances allowed their free movement about the ship. Some sails were torn, while others were shredded. Masts and rigging had snapped, and special details of ship's carpenters were at work repairing leaks that had sprung in the hull. Some of the soldiers were put to work clearing the decks of piles of nasty seaweed and other debris that the giant waves had tossed onto the ship.

Some sense of order was restored quickly, even though the *Spring* had been crippled and remained in such state until the sails were patched or replaced. Other ships in the convoy had experienced a similar fate and were also undergoing needed repairs to keep them afloat and on schedule.

It had been a week of horror at sea, the likes of which none of the soldiers had ever experienced. There were sighs of relief when the sea subsided and the sun finally appeared. Words of thanks were spoken for having been saved. The nightmare was over for sure when codfish in abundant numbers were sighted. Everyone knew then that fish would be on the menu.

Few realized how much seawater had poured into the lower holds, spoiling much of our food supplies. Some were on the verge of rotting. The bedding had also received some unwanted wetting down, and had to be brought on deck to dry out and to rid the mattresses of their musty smell.

I helped where I could, sometimes stowing belongings on dry surfaces, or sweeping compartment floors, or even untangling ropes on deck. The latter was perhaps the hardest and most difficult job for a young person, but at least I was able to breathe the fresh air that was blowing across the ship, rather than inhale the stale and putrid air below.

When my father showed up at mealtime, we all hugged and gave thanks that we were still alive and could hold each other. Mother shed a tear, and said, "Dear Lord, let's not make us go through this again."

I picked up on it right away, saying: "Then we'd have to stay in the British colonies in North America. You wouldn't want to do that, would you?"

"Oh Peter," she replied, "I didn't mean it that way. Of course, we all want to get back home and to the farm."

Papa added, "I'm not one to get scared so easy, but this experience is not one I'd like to repeat if I can avoid it. Staying in North America is pretty much out of the question for me anyway. I am a soldier and I must go where our Prince sends me. So for now, let's try to forget this awful week. You know, we are the lucky ones. Word has it that the ship, *Malaga*, went down at night in the middle of the roughest part of the storm. The ship, its cargo and all souls aboard were lost to the raging sea. It had taken its toll. We pray for them and thank God at the same time for saving us so we can live for another day."

Mother asked, "You mean to tell me the convoy actually lost a ship with everything on it?"

"Yes. Hardly imaginable, but it happened," Papa replied. "Our captain never thought such would be the fate of any of the ships in the convoy. He just shook his head in disbelief as he spoke of the mishap at a staff meeting this morning. A man of war sailed about the area where the ship was lost, but they couldn't find a trace. All debris had disappeared."

He continued, "Even though we are not yet at the true point of no return – the actual halfway point of our voyage – having gone through such unbelievably horrible weather is sufficient for not wanting to turn back. We would have to fear re-visiting the experiences of the past week again. In my mind, I have passed my point of no return. To me, the weather can't get any worse from here on in, and what we might expect at our final destination in the colonies is something I as a soldier do not fear. After all, whatever we encounter there will have to be dealt with according to the circumstances, and whatever it takes to restore or maintain order in the King's name."

Just then, someone shouted, "Man overboard!" Sailors and soldiers were frantically running about, my father among them, to find out just what had happened and assist if help was needed. When he returned, he told us that a sailor who was repairing the rigging near the crow's nest, high up the mast, had lost his grip and fell into the sea. Although many eyes had been scanning the water trying to spot him, he was never seen again. The next day, a brief service in memory of the lost sailor was held topside by Chaplain Hofmeister.

In light of some near-collisions during the storm, the admiral signaled the ships to maintain safe distances from one another. He did this in anticipation of some heavy fog, which he estimated would appear in our path before long. He had acted on his past experience, for no more than two days went by before the convoy was engulfed in a bank of thick fog, impenetrable to the eye. Even though the *Spring* sailed with extreme caution with lookouts at bow and stern, as well as in the crow's nest, and additional listeners and lookouts posted on the decks, the *Spring* hit the side of a nearby transport. The damage assessment detail concluded that immediate repairs would prevent the ship from sinking, and ship's carpenters went to work to repair the damage. It took almost three days before the fog dissipated and the convoy captains again gained a clear view of their surroundings. By this time, the ships were no longer in convoy formation. They were scattered widely from horizon to horizon. Hours later, the admiral signaled that all was well again, and that the convoy should move along with the ships maintaining a safe distance from each other.

On June 1, the King's birthday, the ships of the convoy raised their flags and the escorting men of war fired salvos of salutes in his honor. The day was fine and past hardships seemed forgotten. Hearing and seeing the cannon fire was also exciting. It was something I had not witnessed before. Word of this exercise had been passed among the troops and their dependents only a short time before the ceremonies actually began. I had been preoccupied with everything else, and failed to get the message. Mother was with me on deck as they raised and unfurled the flags, while the sailors and soldiers stood at attention in formation. She, too, enjoyed the moment. Of course, seeing Papa directing his small detachment of Hessian color guards made our faces light up in admiration of our own soldiers. I was watching the exercises closely when I turned to my mother and said, "Look at Papa, isn't he a smart soldier? I didn't know he could shout such loud orders to his men as he just did. That's kind of scary being yelled at like that. But I guess he has to be loud for everyone to hear him. Actually, he sounds just like the Landgrave did when we were at the castle in Marburg and he was drilling his men. Oh yes, and I marched along to the orders he shouted and thought nothing of it at the time. I think it seems more threatening when you are watching from the outside, but to the soldiers, such yelling and shouting apparently is routine."

"Well, son, once you become a drummer, you, too, will be subject to the orders the officers will be shouting. You better get used to it or accept such behavior as normal, lest you regret it later. I just want to be sure you know what you are doing and what you are getting into. After all, you are my son and my best one at that," Mother responded.

"Your best and only son," I uttered.

On one occasion in mid-June, when Papa met with us, he told of a forthcoming baptism ceremony for some of the sailors on board.

"Will they be using Chaplain Hofmeister?" Mother asked.

"Oh, no. This is not a church or religious baptism. There is a tradition among seafarers, that sailors crossing the equator or certain meridians for the first time are baptized in the name of Neptune, the Ruler of the Sea. These sailors are initiated in salt water and are then accepted into the Royal Order of Atlantic Voyagers. Of course, they must pay their dues, with each one of them paying for a half measure of brandy. Hope they have a sufficient number of sailors to initiate so there'll be enough brandy to go around. This might be the only time you will ever see this, Peter. So watch what's going on. You'll want to be able to tell others someday, when we are back home again."

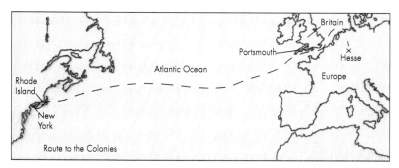

Route to the Colonies

"Papa," I said, "I am so glad you took us along. This trip is a real adventure. We have seen so many new and different things and places, there is just so much. I hope I don't forget half of it before we go back. Who knows what lies ahead on the ocean and once we have landed in the colonies. How much longer will it take before we get to America?"

"Well, son," he said. "We are about one third of the way across. The way I figure it, we left early in May; now it's mid-June and we have two more months to go. Yes, eight weeks or thereabouts. I'm sure we will encounter more rough seas and a few more storms before we can breathe a complete sigh of relief. I am sure we'll do all right. If we got through the last one, we should get through anything else Neptune may decide to place in our path. Maybe after baptizing some of our people in his honor, he will let up on us and allow us smooth sailing. Let's hope so, anyway."

By then, the ship's routine was back to normal. One could tell since the soldiers were forever drilling on the upper deck, weather permitting. And if not there, then down below in one of the holds where there was room between the stacks of stored materials. Of course, I could always be found where the soldiers were. I watched every move they made, wanting to remember exactly how they executed the orders that were given, or better yet, that were shouted.

The next time Papa was with us, he just had to tell how he and his men had been chasing rats down in the bottom hold, where some of the sea water from the gigantic waves had been trapped. Many burlap bags containing flour and other staples had rotted in the dampness, and rats were having a feast at everyone's expense. Mold was forming, and the air smelled sour, like flour paste, bringing on headaches among his men.

"That was a real messy job down there. We got all that sticky and gooey gunk on our uniforms; now we have to give them a good scrubbing. Some of the men were chasing the vermin on hands and knees in the murky water. Funny, but it was really nothing to laugh about. It was a time when soldiers lost their tempers. They were beginning to sound like pirates," he said.

Mother and I looked at each other in disbelief.

"Rats, you mean there are rats just a deck or two below us? That's worse than anything we ever experienced on the farm back home," Mother commented.

"Why didn't you shoot them?" I asked.

"You can't fire a musket at a rat, they move too fast. Besides, we'd get into trouble with the ship's captain if we were to start firing below deck. That wouldn't go over too well. No, we just had to keep trying to corner them one by one, and take care of them in other ways," Papa responded.

"Because of the mess down there," he continued, "the galley will start serving up some biscuits. They tell me the containers in which they are stored are old and have been down in the hold as an emergency supply for many years. Right now, I have no desire to find out what they look or taste like. Maybe they, too, are mildewed. Maybe they've even fallen apart. We might actually experience a real miserable end to our long journey. Oh, and before I forget, our supply of drinking water isn't much better. It's in barrels, but pretty discolored by now, and the taste is awful; it actually stinks. But it's water, and we need to drink water. So, hold your nostrils and drink, that's about all I can say. Keep in mind that each day brings us closer to the colonies, where things should be a lot better," he concluded.

His assessment of the situation was correct. The meals produced in the galley during the last leg of the journey were objectionable and lacking in many respects. To top it off, all of the fresh fruit had been consumed, and the grease used in making our soup had turned rancid. From time to time, a cooked maggot could be seen floating around in the broth, another upsetting interlude to the sad story.

CHAPTER 14

America!

Despite the many hardships the soldiers suffered, they were overjoyed when the lookout shouted "Land Ho!" on August 10. He had spotted the shore near Sandy Hook. It seemed as though everyone had gathered on the upper deck to view the coast, while giving thanks for a safe journey that was coming to a rapid and long-awaited conclusion. Two days later, on August 12, 1776, the convoy anchored off Staten Island. Soon after, disembarking operations got underway.

Our family had a chance to see each other one more time before Papa's unit was shuttled to the shore in long row boats powered by some of the Navy's strongest muscle men.

Prior to the farewells, Papa said, "Well, here we are at the end this exciting journey. It is hard to believe that we were underway for 14 weeks. In that time, we traveled some 3,000 miles. That indeed is an accomplishment no one from Kirchdorf can match. I will disembark shortly with elements of my regiment. We have been given the task of securing the island. The ships will bring the tents and other equipment to the landing dock so we can set up camp in short order. You will be staying on board a few days longer until the regiment is ready to receive and care for you and the other dependents. At that time, you will be able to disembark on the island. I'll see you there after your arrival. Just be patient a few days more, and all will fall in place as planned. Peter, you may not know this yet, but Mother told me she finished up your uniform a few days ago. That means you will get to try it on once you are settled on the island. But listen to me: Don't pester her about the uniform. She will be busy doing chores that the regiment will assign to her. That comes first. Understand? I want to be there when you try on the uniform, so you must be patient a little longer."

"Oh Papa, I am so happy. Mother is the best in the world, in the whole world. I knew all along that you were working on the uniform, Mother. But I never really saw you doing it, even as I tried to catch a glimpse here and there. You know, you were very sneaky about it, but I love you anyway. And Papa, I promise I will not pester her about trying on the uniform until we meet with you on Staten Island. Maybe Captain Feller, the bandmaster, will allow me to begin practicing. I'll be 10 in two months, you know."

"Young man," Papa responded. "For now, just relax a bit. I will tell you when you can join Captain Feller's group for practice. That decision is up to him and me, and I'm telling you to wait!"

"Yes, Papa, I'm just so excited. I can't wait to put the uniform on and start beating the drum."

"Peter, I am sure your father and the captain will insist on more than just beating a drum to your heart's content. I am certain you will have to learn a few things about marching music and military rhythm before being allowed to set the pace for the soldiers," Mother advised.

"I know a lot about that already. I have been watching the soldiers every day, finding out just what they were doing and what the marching and drilling was all about," I replied.

"Son, I am impressed with the interest you have shown, but you must realize that soldiering requires much training. So, you will be spending some time learning precise movements and practices, like any soldier must. When you are done, you will know what to do when certain commands are given. Above all, you will learn how to execute such orders quickly, and with precision. I know you will make us proud by being another member of the Bauer family in the regiment," Papa noted.

"Well, you two," he said. "I must leave you once more. The next time we meet will be on solid ground on one of the King's possessions in North America. It is hard to believe that we finally made it across the ocean after being bounced around aboard ship for weeks on end, often not knowing if we would see another day.

And now, here we are, safe and sound. To be sure, someone was watching over us. We ought to be thankful."

Papa then hugged Mama, and gave me a friendly slap on the shoulder as he turned away to rejoin his men, who had lined up on deck, waiting for further orders. Soon, the men climbed over the side on rope ladders, lowering themselves into smaller boats that were waiting below in the water. The sailors then rowed them to the shore.

Mother and I watched the operation from a safe spot on deck where we would not be in anyone's way. Some of the other children had also come on deck with their mothers to watch as their fathers left the ship to be transported the short distance to Staten Island. Everyone around us seemed happy knowing that they, too, would soon be able to put their feet on solid ground.

After the troops departed, the captain maneuvered closer to shore, where he struck the ship's sails and lowered the anchor, a sign that the *Spring* would just sit there a while.

Two days later, the anchors were hauled early in the morning, and the ship began moving slowly toward the two docks on the island. When they secured the ship, they immediately began unloading its cargo. Down below, the soldiers that had landed earlier were waiting to receive their wagons, some loaded with tents and related gear, so they could begin setting up the regiment's camp. It took a whole two days for all the supplies and equipment to be discharged. That done, one of the ship's officers holding a list of passengers, checked off the names of women and children as we left for the island by way of a gangplank. Out of courtesy to the women, the officer gave the group a final salute as we departed.

"There he is. There's Papa!" I yelled the minute I spotted him among a group of soldiers waiting below on the dock.

"Papa, Papa, here we are!" I continued shouting.

"Oh, Peter. He has seen us and is waving his hands," Mother said, trying to calm me down and curb my extreme enthusiasm.

"Hello, you two," was his greeting as we set foot on ground.

"Welcome to Staten Island and the King's colonies," he continued. "Let me help you with your bag, Anna, and we'll head straight for the camp and your tent where you can make yourselves at home. I imagine you will be staying here for a while, certainly while most of the regiment will be in the field, securing other areas for the King. There is word out that our unit may head for Long Island with the British soon. We might have to go by boat, I don't know yet. But, you'll be staying here until we return or until the remainder of the regiment and you, are ordered to follow. We'll have to wait that out."

As we were walking away from the dock, Mother inquired, "Do you mean you will be heading into uncharted territory?"

"It's not uncharted in the sense that we have maps and the terrain is friendly, but we do not know how the colonists will accept our presence. They have become unruly and rebellious in other quarters. Now we have to find out what the local attitude is. If they have a militia under arms, we want to be sure they are friendly. If not, we'll try to get them to disarm. If that doesn't work, we'll have to convince them to do so by showing our strength in numbers and weapons," he replied.

"Papa," I said. "Do you think they will stand up and fight and make you shoot?"

"Can't say. I hope not. We'd rather be friends with the colonists. They haven't hurt any of us. Their arguments are with the King. Problem is, our Prince has agreed to have us Hessians assist the King's men in whatever their mission may be here in the colonies. We could be fighting whether we like it or not. What our real role will be depends to a large extent on the behavior and attitude of the colonists," he concluded.

When we arrived at the camp, the supply officer and quartermaster, Lieutenant Schmitt, showed us to our assigned tent. Our personal belongings were sitting in the tent waiting for us. Papa thanked the officer for having had our belongings brought to the tent in advance of our arrival, which made it easier for us to settle in for our first night in North America.

The next morning Mother was summoned to assist the regimental doctor and his small team in taking care of sick soldiers. She was told that the cause for their illnesses might be found in the poor food they had received during the last few weeks aboard ship. Some of the men were dehydrated; others were struggling with excessive weight loss, while others had pains in their stomachs. Mother and several other women worked hard feeding and caring for the ill, and assisting the doctor. Theirs were not pleasant jobs, but they wanted to do all they could to help the soldiers regain their health.

About the same time the women were put to work, Major Albrecht of the Prinz Carl Regiment, a former visiting professor at the University of Marburg, made a point of ordering the children back to school rather than allowing them to sit about doing little to enhance their knowledge. Together with the field parson, they developed a worthy program of education that fit their student body. The major took the drummer boys from the several regiments on the island in tow, including myself, even though I had not yet been accepted. He wanted to help us develop an ability to read music, a priority on his list of subjects to be taught. In addition, he concentrated on teaching us drummers how to read, write and compose reports on our activities, a prerequisite for young Hessian auxiliary members.

On August 21, Papa spoke with us briefly, advising that most of his regiment had been directed to join a British task force, along with other Hessian troops, for an attack in the direction of Long Island.

We later learned that Sir William Howe had ordered a landing in Flatbush, where stiff opposition was encountered. Some five days later, the local militia had been outflanked and taken prisoner. The remainder of the enemy retreated toward Brooklyn during the night. Howe's campaign continued into September, when Manhattan was invaded by a combined British-Hessian force, resulting in the retreat of opposing forces to Fort Washington in upper Manhattan.

Although the victorious British-Hessian forces marched into the city of New York with drums beating and flags flying, the local population was less than enthusiastic at their coming. Four days later, a large fire broke out in Manhattan, destroying nearly half of the houses, including the Lutheran and Trinity churches. No one knew how the fire began. However, the British felt that American patriots had kindled the raging inferno.

During the period of these operations, life on Staten Island continued at a normal pace. We drummer boys were diligently pursuing our studies under Major Albrecht. Luckily, he, too, was able to stay behind when most of the men in his regiment moved out as part of Howe's march on Long Island. Most of the men who had been in the infirmary or otherwise under the doctor's care had been healed and were allowed to resume normal duties. Mama and the women were busy preparing bandages and other medical supplies, waiting to care for the wounded that would be brought back from the fighting on Long Island and Manhattan.

To prepare the drummers for our future roles, Major Albrecht devoted some time to explaining military habits and courtesies to us boys, most older than myself, but just as unskilled as I was in military ways. As part of the military educational process, he insisted we address him as 'sir.' In turn, he referred to our boys as 'junge' – boy – and sometimes, 'trommelbube' – drummer boy.

After the fire in New York, Papa and some of his men were relieved from the fighting and returned to Staten Island, with a like number of replacements taking their places in the city.

"It was murder," he told us when he returned to the island.

"I am disappointed at having to fight the colonists, but they took up arms against the King, their sovereign. That makes them rebels in the true sense of the word, and we had no alternative but to put them down. There were many wounded on both sides. Some of our men were bandaged up on the field. A few died. Others were moved out of the battle area and will be brought back here for proper treatment. So you better get ready, Anna. Of course, the battlefield dead were buried with honors near where they had fallen. It is a pity that their lives had to end so far from their homes and families. Our officers will send condolences to their next of kin. Still, it is a sad way to die, but a soldier's death is an honorable death. All fulfilled their oath. All died for their Prince."

I then asked, "Did they shoot at you?"

"Son, soldiers doing battle get shot at. The idea is to keep marching and shooting at the enemy without stopping. Soldiers say their prayers when they march on the enemy. They actually march into their musket fire, hoping to gain ground and fire at the opponent before he can re-load. Much is having faith, combined with being lucky. I am here. I made it fine, and we were being shot at. They were not fighting like soldiers. At times, they were hiding behind stone walls or large trees instead of coming out into the open and facing us head-on, as good soldiers do."

"Karl," Mother inquired, "Do you think there will be many more confrontations? All of this worries me. I figured there might be some minor resistance, but you have faced some tough opponents. There has been word that they have a general by the name of Washington leading them and that he has gathered a whole army of supporters."

"What you are not aware of, Anna, is that our General Heister has greater skills and experience than their man Washington. Heister is an old soldier, a real fox and no one is going to trump him. Wait and see. As far as future engagements we may encounter, that's something we can't predict. We have to face things as they develop."

"How about it, Peter, how are you doing?" he continued. "How's school?"

"I'm doing well," I replied. "Major Albrecht is treating us like soldiers. Gosh, Papa, he is strict, but we are learning a lot from him."

"Your birthday is on October 10, and you'll finally be 10. That's your magic number. You need to be 10 before Captain Max Feller, our bandmaster will enroll you as a regimental drummer boy at the pleasure of Colonel Lossberg, the commander. Well, I'll talk with him in a day or two. If he has authority to approve your acceptance on your birthday, then that would indeed be a time to celebrate."

"Thank you, Papa. I've been waiting for this. When can I try on the uniform? I'd like to try it on to make sure it fits."

"Well, maybe you can try it on the next time I come to see the two of you. That might be in a few days. What do you think, Anna?"

"Of course. That's fine with me. I'll get it all together to make sure everything is done, and then I'll iron it so Peter can try it on when you stop by."

In the meantime, wounded Hessian soldiers were brought to Staten Island for treatment by Hessian doctors, as agreed by Britain's King George III and the Landgrave of Hesse. My mother,

Bertha Meyer, wife of the supply sergeant, and Lotte Weinfeld, wife of the armorer, worked as a team in the medical facility which consisted of several tents at the edge of the Staten Island encampment. My mother told me that several of the convalescing soldiers were detailed to assist the medical team. Among their duties was hauling barrels of fresh water by horse-drawn wagon, and cleaning up the insides of the medical tents.

When Papa visited a few days later, Mother brought out the uniform. My eyes almost popped out of their sockets. I saw what had long been the object of my wishes. Now that it was before me, it became an unimaginable reality. I stood there holding my breath in anticipation, trying to hold back a tear in humble appreciation for what my mother had done for me.

"Oh, Mother!" I cried. "I'm so sorry for ever having nagged and doubted you. Please forgive me. I love you so much. And Papa, I can't thank you enough for encouraging me and helping me along, and for talking to the people who make a difference. Can I put it on now? Do you think I will look like a real soldier?"

"Go on, son. Try on the uniform. Let's see if you can be identified as a member of the Ditfurth Regiment," Papa suggested.

It didn't take long for me to change and put on my new duds – a brand-new uniform. My own mother had actually made it just for me. When I stepped out in front of our tent, both of my parents nodded in approval, telling me how fine I looked. Yes, I did look much like a soldier, only a bit shorter. I hadn't reached five feet yet, while most of the regulars were close to six feet tall. In addition, the men in the regiment wore pointed helmets, making them look even taller. I was given a three-cornered black hat adorned with a white pompom. As a drummer, I also wore large striped epaulettes, called Schwalbennester – swallows nests – on my shoulders. These identified me as a musician and member of the band; in my case, as a drummer. I know I looked smart and made a good impression, strutting around before my father and mother with a big grin of satisfaction on my face.

"You make a fine-looking soldier, Peter," Papa said. "Now you have to train to become one. You'll hear from the bandmaster as soon as he can spend some time with you to explain some of the military rituals and show you how to use the drum not only for marching, but also as an instrument to send signals to others."

"What do you mean using the drum as a signaling instrument?" I asked.

"In the field, orders are sometimes relayed by way of certain pre-arranged drum beats that are known to our officers and a few subordinates, like move forward, fall back, hold positions, retreat," my father explained.

"I didn't know that," I replied.

"Well, son, that's why you have to be trained. So you can understand and do these things without having someone whisper into your ear at a time when your signals are critical to the success of an operation. Always remember, the drummer is a very important element in any unit and in any campaign. Success or failure often rests squarely on the drummer's shoulders."

In mid-October, after I had my tenth birthday, I was accepted as a newcomer to the regimental band, destined to become their newest drummer boy. Papa had presented me to the bandmaster, with me wearing my uniform with great pride. There was little ceremony since my acceptance had been previously discussed. The only thing holding up the actual enrollment had been my age, since the colonel's approval had been obtained earlier. When I met the minimum age requirement, there were no further questions or hurdles to overcome. I remained with the bandmaster for a private lesson when my father returned to his own unit.

Life became more rigorous for me, despite my young age, having to train like any soldier. In marching, I often took two steps to every one by the soldiers. When the sergeant noticed this, he coached me to take longer steps so the cadence was uniform. Overall, I was in a good position since I could actually set a slower pace with my drum, especially after longer marches that tired me out, unless I was ordered to speed it up. Generally, the Hessians marched at a slow, but deliberate pace, not like the colonists, who always seemed in a hurry. Their drums often set their pace at quick time, a much faster marching rate – almost like running.

The lessons I had to take included various exercises, including drumming patterns, rhythms, beats to set cadence, roll of drums, ruffles and signals to summon troops, relay orders, and more. I performed the assignments very seriously, having been impressed with the critical responsibilities of my position. And, just as I was beginning to understand my instrument, the job and the array of orders that could be barked at me during given situations, Papa told us that six Hessian regiments would join an equal number of British units to establish a garrison in Newport, Rhode Island.

"We're on the go, again," he told Mother and me when he saw us. "I guess we can't call Staten Island our home for any prolonged period of time, as I had hoped.

"Captain von Schwetzingen alerted our unit, advising us to start packing and prepare to embark on one of the 70 or so ships the British are assembling for the expedition to Newport. The operation will be headed up by their General Clinton. Lord Percy will accompany him. We still have a week or so to prepare, but I'm told they are planning to sail from New York no later than December 1, 1776."

"What will happen to us, Karl?" Mother asked.

"Oh, I almost forgot to tell you, the dependents are coming with us. You'll have to excuse me for not having mentioned that right away. I have so many things on my mind with the unit's packing and loading that I am beginning to forget the things that are of real importance to me personally," he replied.

"Will I be going with the unit as their drummer, or will I have to stand by idly?" I asked.

"Well, Peter, you just recently started your training. There is still much more to be learned before you can accompany any of the units in the field. But, I imagine you will be allowed to participate in some marching formations to begin with, once we get settled in Newport. You may as well prepare yourself for something like that. You know, once you have completed your training, it could happen that the regiment might even assign you to another unit temporarily, should one of their regular drummers drop out for some reason," Papa noted.

"Oh gosh, drumming for another regiment with different officers and men? I thought I'd stay with the Ditfurth Regiment where you are. I suppose they could even assign me to a different sector, right, Papa?"

"That could be, Peter. All depends on the situation and who gets assigned to do what."

"Karl, how do you envision our stay in the Newport area?" Mother asked.

"Well, Anna. Initially, most of us, you included, will have to make do with living and sleeping in a tent. And as soon as adequate facilities can be acquired, you will be moved into more permanent quarters. You, Anna, will always be near the regiment's operational area; after all, we couldn't do without you," he replied.

"Oh sure, you fellows need me alright. I bet some of your people feel we are more of a hinderance to you than anything else," she responded.

"Not so, everyone knows just how much our women are doing for us. Just think about it. You assist the medical people, make bandages, care for the wounded, clean the area of the infirmary, speak encouraging words to lonely soldiers and to top it off, you help with the cooking and feeding. Oh yes, and let's not forget that you teach the children and also do tailoring work. To me, that's a big bundle of work we can't do without. So, take a bow, Anna, be proud of yourself. You are well appreciated, wanted and needed. Besides, you have to function as both parents from time to time. Peter depends on you a great deal, even more so when I am not around. And the way I see it, I may well be somewhere in the field, patrolling a good deal of the time."

Mama smiled at hearing such appreciative words coming from Papa, which was an unusual occurrence under present circumstances. I knew Mother could use some encouragement and praise, especially since all the attention in recent times had focused on Papa and me. Then, she knew that her contributions and efforts were noticed and acknowledged.

Papa then suggested that we begin packing, so we would be ready when called. As expected, he said his farewells and headed for the troop encampment to get his men ready for the move.

CHAPTER 15

Newport and Rhode Island

The expedition to Newport got underway on December 1, as planned. It was a clear day as the convoy headed north in calm waters. Although I had been enrolled as a drummer of the Ditfurth Regiment, I was advised to travel in the company of my mother, rather than be billeted with the soldiers. Luckily, my father was on the same ship with his detachment of men. Once in open waters, it did not take long for him to catch up with Mama and me, his regiment's new drummer boy.

"Hello, you two. How are you today? Hope the boarding went well and someone helped with your belongings. My captain had assigned me to oversee the movement of our personnel since we were allotted two ships and had to split up our people. My job was to ensure the people stayed with their unit and got on the ship to which they had been assigned. No matter how hard you try, there is always someone who doesn't listen and gets fouled up. This time was no different. One of the men from Lieutenant Schmitt's quartermaster unit somehow was among my men as they were about to head up the gangplank. Luckily, I spotted him and called him out of the line. Otherwise, Lieutenant Schmitt would have reported one of his men missing. But, that's our way of life. Never a dull moment."

"Karl, that is a lot of responsibility you have, sorting out who's who. You must have to know the people pretty well to do that efficiently. You can't afford to make any mistakes," Mother responded.

"Well, Anna, we are soldiers, and what I am doing is part of my job. As soldiers, we cannot afford to make mistakes. There is too much at risk. It's just like not wanting to lose a sheep. But, if we do and bring it back, we rejoice at finding or saving one of our own."

"Papa," I mumbled. "It's pretty cold out here in open waters. You said we would have to sleep in tents right after we land in Rhode Island? Won't it be too cold to be outside like that?"

"Ha, it might be cold and uncomfortable for a few nights, but we have to scout out the town of Newport first to see where we might be able to billet the men of the regiment as well as our dependents, you included. I am pretty sure we'll be able to move the two of you into one of the buildings in or near the town very quickly. None of us want to leave our family members without knowing they are taken care of," he replied.

"What do you mean leaving us?" I queried.

"As I mentioned the other day, the regiment will be patrolling Rhode Island as a matter of routine to insure we are all safe. We haven't met up with the colonists in Newport yet, so we don't know how they feel about us. Much depends on their attitude. If they are friendly, we might be able to relax our vigil a bit, but if

they are hostile and opposed to our presence, behaving in an arbitrary manner, then of course, we have to tighten up our security and increase our patrols. So you see, Peter, it's hard to predict when I'll be able to be nearby."

"I understand," I replied.

Except for encountering a single renegade ship that opened fire on one of the transports but was quickly disabled by the guns of a nearby British man of war, the seven-day sail to the entrance of Narragansett Bay in Rhode Island was uneventful.

The convoy sailed into the bay by way of the West Passage to avoid any possible gunfire from Newport, using Conanicut Island as a protective shield. Passing along the western shore of the island, an observer spotted earthworks about a mile north of the island's southern tip. While the ships proceeded with caution and the men of war kept their guns loaded and ready to fire, no activity was noticed about the defensive works ashore. Entry into the bay at the north end of Conanicut proceeded without interference, to our relief.

We were told the admiral had ordered the disembarkation to proceed swiftly. The objective was to shuttle a fighting force to the shore early in the day to quickly secure Newport, which would allow the transports to draw closer to the town's docks for unloading of critical cargo. The initial landings in the town were made by British troops, while our Hessians came ashore farther north at Weaver's Cove.

Despite their best efforts, the ships were unable to discharge their cargo in time for any tents to be set up before nightfall. To top it off, the weather had changed dramatically during the time of the landing operation. Large amounts of snow were falling, which prompted General Clinton to call off any further operations until the next morning. Meanwhile, the troops on shore spent their first night sleeping on the ground, using their blankets to protect themselves from the drifting snow. Nonetheless, scouting parties were sent northward on Aquidneck Island, where no local opposition was encountered. The troops that remained aboard the transports, and dependents like ourselves, were fortunate to spend another night in the warm, though smelly environment of their ships.

By the time our family and the remaining dependents were brought ashore two days later, several houses on Thames Street, from whence the owners had fled, had been taken over as quarters for British and Hessian personnel. After Papa quartered the men of his detail in one of the buildings, he set out to locate us, not sure if we had found shelter somewhere along Thames Street or nearby. He found Mother in one of the houses that had been taken over. She told him we could keep warm, as long as we were supplied with an adequate quantity of firewood.

"Anna, firewood is scarce. I have been allocated a quarter cord of wood weekly, plus one cord for each detail of 12 men, as well as a limited amount of candles and several bushels of coal per cord of wood. It might sound like a lot, but none of it lasts very long. We are already talking about gathering firewood elsewhere by sending details to more remote areas by ship to harvest the needed wood for the garrison. We are also looking at decaying buildings, like old barns, even wooden fences and posts as possible sources to fulfill our needs for fuel. Only time will tell how far we have to go. By the way, where is Peter?"

"You won't believe it, Karl," she replied "He is over at the British-Hessian Brigade Headquarters. You know, the town house, hanging around with the guard detachment, waiting for the officer to call a formation for which he might be the drummer. Some of the boys from the other regiments are there, too. They are trying to outdo each other, so they're beating the drums feverishly at times. I imagine they must disturb your headquarters personnel with all that racket. And then, they have been marching around the parade area in front of the building, setting the marching pace for themselves and the soldiers who are out there drilling."

"I'm glad he is doing well now that a drum has been entrusted to his care. This will teach him responsibility. The drum has to be kept clean and maintained for it to be presentable and to give off the right sound. Everyone knows the Hessians are coming by the sound of our drums, which produce a very deep tone. It makes some people nervous. Some actually perceive our drumbeats as threatening," he said.

"And," he continued, "I wanted you to know that my detachment, along with several other units, will move into the field soon. We will march to Portsmouth to set up camp and patrol the shore facing Tiverton where the Continental Militia is said to be gathering. We need to find out what they are up to. I hope they don't plan on landing on our side. Unless they come to surrender, we'll have to confront them with loaded muskets, which is not very desirable. And since we only have a reconnaissance mission with no fighting anticipated or projected, we might just take Peter along to give him his first marching experience in the field."

When I returned home that night, Mother broke the news to me that I might be joining my father's unit on a reconnaissance mission to Portsmouth. Hearing what I perceived as 'the good news,' I hugged my mother, and told her I would be careful and not to worry.

During the intervening days, there were two primary duties for me to perform: attend the daily school classes that were prescribed for all dependent children, and participate in the practice sessions of the band and the drills of the marching units. By so doing, I became well versed in executing the various commands our superiors would be giving to the marching columns. I marched and beat the drum at the pace set by the drilling officer. The commands given by the Landgrave during the drill back home rang out like a bell in my mind: "Achtung," "Vorwärts marsch," "Abteilung halt," – attention, forward march and detail halt. These were terms I had heard before. All had meant something to me even before I was enrolled as a regimental drummer boy. I felt very comfortable in the tough military environment, and I was beginning to like soldiering better each day.

Moving into field positions was delayed. The Ditfurth Regiment remained in Newport until the weather broke, and members of the von Huyn Regiment that had bivouaced in the countryside on the north end of Aquidneck returned to town early in 1777. In March, the regiment was finally ordered to take over the positions that had been vacated. It was anticipated that we would be staying in the field for a month or more depending on circumstances.

On the day members of the regiment were about to proceed into the countryside to take up their positions, Papa stopped by quickly to say farewell to Mother, who hated to see him go.

Since I was one of the regiment's drummer boys, I also came around to let my mother know I would be going with the group of Hessians. During this awkward moment of farewells, Papa told me, "Believe it or not, by the time you return to Newport, the wagon master will have refurbished your drum. Your own drum, that is. You can thank Captain Feller, the bandmaster, for letting you use one of his spare drums for now, but before long you will have to return it and use your own. The wagon master hadn't forgotten the waterlogged drum you dragged from the river. Remember? As promised, he located the needed materials to make the repairs. I'd say, you are among the very lucky people around here. Let's hope for the best while we are in Portsmouth, and we should all be back before you know it."

"I thought the wagon master might have forgotten that he wanted to try to rebuild my drum, but I guess he hadn't. It'll be nice to have my own drum. I won't have to be so overcautious in handling it as I must with the one Captain Feller loaned me," I responded.

"Well, now. Just because the drum will be yours doesn't mean you can bang it around, you know. It still belongs to the regiment. It will be in your custody and it will be your responsibility to take care of it, just like your own clothes, understand?"

"Yes, Papa. I only meant I'll feel much better knowing I have my own drum instead of one that's on loan to me. I just feel different about it," I replied.

"I can see where you would be more at ease with your own drum," Mother added.

My father and I left together after each of us had given Mother another great big hug. She stood there, saddened at our departure, yet she was smiling with pride and waving at us as we headed down the street to join the formation of soldiers that had assembled on the parade ground in front of Newport's Colony House.

Soon, officers began shouting orders and the troops came to attention. After some additional details were given in voices loud enough for everyone to hear, the column of some 100 soldiers stepped off in a northerly direction. I and another drummer a few years older than me were marching in front of the line, beating our drums to set the pace for the soldiers. After two hours, my legs began to hurt from all that marching. Luckily, the troops were given a short break before continuing their trek that eventually ended at Butts Hill, or Windmill Hill, as the Hessians called it. The

site consisted of a large earthworks the colonists had built and within its protective parapets stood a wooden structure sufficient to house some 60 or so soldiers.

My father and his detachment were among the ones staying at Butts Hill. The remaining 40, me included, were directed to proceed farther north and eastward across open fields until we reached a small fresh water creek, where we could pitch tents while maintaining a defensive position. This was essential, since our presence could be observed from across the water in Tiverton, where large numbers of colonists and rebel militia were said to be assembling.

After dark, I crawled into my tent and snuggled around my drum, holding it tight with both arms, making sure no one could take it during the night. Like everyone else, I slept in my clothes. I had learned earlier that shoes quickly absorb the cold while asleep and transmit the chill through the body. I took them off for the night, but to insure they would still be there in the morning, I used them as a pillow to rest my head. At five in the morning, Sergeant Hurler of our detail woke me by pulling at my feet.

"Time to wake up, soldier. Go wash up in the creek and get back here quickly. We'll be making some hot coffee to go with some biscuits we brought along. Hurry," he said.

"Thanks, sergeant. It's chilly this morning. The ground was real cold during the night, even with the blanket covering me inside the tent," I replied.

"Well, son, that's the way it is in the army. Hate to say it, but you better get used to it," the sergeant commented.

After the men had cleaned up and had their morning coffee, Sergeant Hurler ordered them to line up in a double column. Lieutenant Wurzburg, the officer in charge of the detail, then addressed the men.

"As you will have noticed, we can see the rebels moving about across the water. And they are watching us at this very moment. I am telling you this to be sure you are alert at all times and pay attention to what is going on around you. Keep an eye on the shore at the bottom of the hill, just below our camp. The enemy may try to land on our side at any time."

"The drummer will stay close to me at all times. On my orders, he will signal you as necessary. All of you know the meaning of the regimental drumbeat alerts. We would most likely signal in the event of a general alert, or perhaps call you to assemble on the drummer's position, where I will be. Sergeant Hurler will head up a 12-man detail that will patrol close to the shoreline. In the event of any action by the dissidents that would indicate a possible move toward our shore, he will send a runner to report the sighting to me. We will rotate the 12-man detail every eight hours, including during times of darkness. Meals will be prepared here in the encampment. Those on patrol at mealtime will receive their portions after they are relieved and return to camp. One final word: We must remain as inconspicuous as possible. They know we are here, but we don't have to let them know how we are deployed, or where everyone is. As long as they remain uncertain of our whereabouts, they won't try anything. Remember that," he said in conclusion.

The days in the field were uneventful, except when influenced by bad weather. While it was a joy to drink refreshing water from the creek and wash up at will, on rainy days, life became miserable, particularly if water entered our tents. Unaware of the consequences, I had touched the wet canvas of my shelter repeatedly from the inside while struggling with my drum in the confined area of the tent. It didn't take long for my blankets and clothes to get soaked from the water that began leaking through the canvas. My major concern, of course, was my drum. I protected it in whatever way I could, keeping it dry even by laying across the instrument while getting wet myself. These problems notwithstanding, I was happy to know that my tent was well staked and anchored solidly to the ground. It would not be blown away when offshore winds suddenly pick up in strength. Those who had failed to stake their tent properly suffered the consequences, which sometimes forced them to abandon their flimsy shelter in the midst of a rainstorm.

Despite inclement weather, the soldiers were expected to keep themselves, their uniforms and their equipment in tip-top shape, always being prepared for inspection on short notice. Anticipating such possibilities, combined with some fear due to inexperience, I cleaned and brushed my equipment and clothes every chance I got. Some of the soldiers laughed when they saw what I was doing, telling me I'd wear out my uniform if I kept brushing it more than once a day. But I didn't let anything bother me. I wasn't going to be called out for looking sloppy like some of the soldiers were.

Several weeks had passed when a detail of soldiers from the von Bünau Regiment relieved us and took over our duties. I could have jumped for joy at the thought of returning to Newport, where our group would again be billeted in houses – places with solid walls that would protect us from nature's elements.

During my time in the field, I often thought of my mother, who had remained in town when our detail from the Ditfurth Regiment headed for our field assignments. Then I would get a chance to see her again. I had also not seen my father since we said good-bye at Butts Hill, and, of course, I was looking forward to meeting him when we rejoined the main body of troops at the earthworks on our way back to Newport.

When Lieutenant Wurzburg gave the marching order for our detail to move out, I began beating my drum with determination. This was a happy time for me. Even though the soldiers had to make their way across meadowland, my drumbeats provided the cadence necessary to make marching easier on the uneven terrain. Once we hit the country road, everyone straightened up and

JHS

fell into proper marching order, knowing we were approaching Butts Hill, where we would meet up with the remainder of our unit.

Who else would be waiting for the approaching detail? None other than my father, Sergeant Bauer. He wanted to observe first-hand how his drummer boy was doing. He told me that watching us come closer with me up front in the line made him feel proud. My uniform that my mother had sewn so diligently for weeks on end looked perfect. I looked sharp, at least that is what I was telling myself. I knew I was a proper trooper of the Ditfurth Regiment. I could feel it.

Our detail marched past the guard at the entrance to the Butts Hill earthworks and onward to the parade ground, when Lieutenant Wurzburg shouted the orders. "Abteilung halt. Rechts um. Rührt Euch." After halting the detail, he ordered a right face, followed by "at ease."

I couldn't wait to shout: "Papa, I'm back. See me and my drum?"

Some of the men were grinning when I called their sergeant,

"Papa." I don't know why some of the younger soldiers would laugh when he could very well have been their papa, too.

"Hello, Peter, I see you. You look just fine," were his first words.

Once dismissed by Lieutenant Wurzburg, I made a mad dash in my father's direction, dragging my drum along.

"Hi Papa, are you alright? Nothing happened near water's edge where we had camped. But we did see a lot of rebels on the opposite shore, just across from our bivouac area. They didn't try coming over, though," I said.

"Things were also quiet here at Butts Hill. We were busy most of the time, building several storage sheds within the perimeter of the earthworks. Oh, and some of the men were making the area inaccessible from the outside by cutting trees down and throwing branches on top of each other, creating impassable obstructions in the likely paths of any attackers. So, now we have a real fort here at Butts Hill, and it is defendable," Papa replied.

He continued, "We will be heading back to town tomorrow. The men of the von Bünau Regiment will sleep in their tents tonight until we clear out. After that, the place is theirs."

At five in the morning, my drum struck the wake-up call for the troops. Most of the men must have been laying awake waiting for the drum call because it didn't take long for them to hustle about to clean up, eat and pack for the march south to Newport. Although I dreaded the long hike ahead, I kept beating away on my drum until our 100-man detail was ordered to stop for a short break. For me, the timing for the short rest period was just right. My legs felt tired by this time and my arms were getting numb from keeping up the drumbeat from the time we left Butts Hill until now. At the order to halt and fall out, I quickly sought out a soft spot in the grass and plunked myself on the ground. I could have fallen asleep, the march had been so strenuous, but the order "Antreten" – fall in – jerked me out of my drowsiness and brought me back to reality. The rest period was over and minutes later I was at it again, setting the pace for the soldiers that followed only a few short feet behind me. To my regret, the second drummer who had accompanied us to the Portsmouth outpost, became ill and had returned to Newport a few days earlier. This made me the

only available and unofficial 'tambour' of the regiment, a position of responsibility I had not anticipated receiving so early in my newfound career as a "shave tail" or novice drummer boy. Realizing the situation I was in, I pulled myself together and marched, and marched, drumming all the way to Newport.

The unit was dismissed on the parade ground in front of the Colony House. Only the officers and sergeants were required to stay behind to file reports of their field experiences and observations. The ordinary soldiers, including me, were dismissed to return to our billets in town. With my drum dangling from my shoulders, I ran all the way to Thames Street and the house we had been assigned. Mother had heard our drumbeats as we paraded to the Colony House and was waiting at the door for her two men to return home.

She greeted me, saying, "Peter, how nice you look. I'm so happy you are back home. Where's your father? You must be hungry, come in, sit down and tell me all about it while I make something to eat for the two of you."

"Mother, I am so glad to be back, and I am so tired. My feet hurt from the long hike back from Portsmouth. I hope I don't have any blisters on my sore feet. My arms are numb, like dead. I have no feeling in them from carrying and beating the drum without much let-up, except for a 15-minute break along the way every now and then. But I am fine – really. Papa is at the Colony House with the officers and the other sergeants. I guess they have to make their reports. He'll be home soon, I am sure. How have you been? Are you all right? Did you miss us? I sure missed you a lot. Sleeping in tents was not my best experience, but I got used to it after a while. I'll know better next time not to touch the canvas when it is wet from the rain. The first time we had a real heavy downpour, I almost drowned in my own tent from all the water that was seeping through. And my clothes were soaked. I hated it and wished I were back in town at our place, right here on Thames Street."

"Well, you sure had some exciting experiences. I imagine you learned a lot during your field assignment," she replied.

"Sure did," I replied.

"You think I could lay down and sleep a while, at least until Papa comes home?"

"Oh sure. Go lay down on the bed, but take off your shoes and accouterments," she replied.

I was still sound asleep when Papa returned home a few hours later.

"Hello, everybody. We are all finally back together again. Isn't it great? Anna, we missed you and your good cooking. How did you hold up with your two men gone all that time?" he asked.

"Well, you fellows should know that I was kept extremely busy working for the regiment while you were away. I didn't think much of your absence until evenings when I was back home alone. Then I wondered what kind of trouble the two of you might have gotten into. We didn't hear much of what was going on up there in Portsmouth. We prayed you were all safe, and that the rebels didn't decide to invade the island while you were out there. Word had been passed, though, that large numbers of armed dissidents were gathering in Tiverton. I wonder what they are up to? We also became somewhat concerned that the British had ordered two of the Hessian regiments transferred elsewhere a few weeks ago. We understand they left by boat without much fanfare. You can rest assured, our prayers were with you for the duration of your field assignment. At least everything worked out well and all of you came back safe and sound, with the exception of the other drummer, who came down with a terrible fever. The poor boy died while at the Hessian medical facility that had been set up in one of the churches. So much for the local news. Now, sit and enjoy a nice home-cooked meal for a change," she concluded.

"I'm sorry that the Prince Carl and DuCorps Regiments were pulled out. From the size of the Continental and Militia units gathering in Tiverton, we certainly would need more troops on our side to successfully ward off any potential attack. Of course,

they would have to come by boat and land on our side first. That should give us a pretty good advantage – dug in and well fortified in the vicinity of Butts Hill. It will allow enough time to call for reinforcements from among our reserves in town. But, their numbers could become overwhelming if they are allowed to get a solid hold on the northern end of our island," Papa commented.

I then asked, "Do you think the British will call in more troops from other places if the rebels invade the island?"

"Can't tell. It would all depend on how large a force they could muster to come ashore up north. Then, there is always a matter of time to be reckoned with; that is, how well and fast the enemy might advance on Newport, what we might do to delay their operations and how long it would take us to bring in more troops from New York. We are talking a week at least to beef up our defenses. That can be a long time when help is needed in a hurry," he answered.

We finally quieted down to savor a real home-cooked meal once again. Mother was delighted to watch us, her "two boys" as she called us, enjoy the food she had prepared. She then joined us and ate a large portion herself. She smiled in satisfaction, knowing it tasted good.

After supper, we all helped clean up and called it a day, bedding down by nightfall.

The next day, the troops in town followed their daily routine of training and doing essential chores required by the garrison. Presently, they were busy gathering up a winter supply of firewood from all over the island. The British went about tearing down abandoned barns and sheds for the same purpose, until they had established several well-stocked wood supply points within the confines of Newport. Later in the year, several incursions were made to islands close to Long Island, where joint British-Hessian work details loaded their ships with wood harvested in those areas in anticipation of the garrison's needs in Newport.

It was September 1777 when Papa told us that Colonel Lossberg, the recently assigned commander of the Ditfurth Regiment, had addressed his troops, telling them that the British Commandant requires the earthworks we spotted on the western shore of Conanicut Island as we entered the bay in the prior year, to be enlarged and reinforced. For this purpose he ordered a work-force of 300 men to embark for the island in a few days. The detail was comprised of British and Hessian personnel at a 50-50 ratio. Captain von Schwetzingen and his unit were assigned to the mission. No rebel encounter or other adverse action was expected on Conanicut Island, but patrols were maintained along the shore at all times.

British and Hessian troops and their officers were rotated periodically at their jobs for the duration of the encampment. Smaller elements of the detail would commence gathering firewood and depositing it at a collection point to be established, to be stored there for later transport to Newport.

A scouting and security detail established a position above the high rocky shore in the area referred to as the Dumplings. Every effort was made to bring us back to Newport before adverse weather set in. For this reason, it was essential that each and every soldier work diligently to complete the assignment with determination.

Two days later, the combined 300-man detail was moved to Conanicut Island aboard a naval transport, where the troops were put ashore in flat boats at the existing ferry landing. While a British advance detail immediately headed for the earthworks at Fox Hill, the troops remaining behind assisted in bringing tents and supplies ashore from the ship that was anchored close by. In the interim, a small group of British soldiers scoured nearby homes and yards for horses and wagons to transport supplies. Over the objections of island residents, three wagons and six horses were requisitioned and used by the Hessian contingent to move their tents and equipment.

With loaded wagons, our Hessians and their British brothers in arms proceeded in a westerly direction, toward the island's crossroad, with me at the head of the column. This was the first time the people on Conanicut Island heard the deep and threatening sound of our Hessian drums, sounds already known too well in the streets of Newport. Despite the continuous "thump, thump, thump-thump-thump," of my drum, the men could hardly keep in step on the bumpy and hilly road. Some were even holding on to a wagon here and there, their marching boots kicking up a dense cloud of dry dust. Drum beats and coughing mixed into a sad melody with the men – dressed in woolen uniforms – perspiring in the heat of the day.

At the crossroads near Battery Park, our column turned left, heading south past the beach where prevailing winds provided a welcoming breeze. All the time, I kept beating my drum as sweat ran down my cheeks. After the column had negotiated the steep hill on the road to Beavertail, a British guard directed us to a narrow path and down a partially overgrown hill to the earthworks, where British soldiers were sitting about, awaiting our arrival.

Unloading the cargo and setting up their tents was a priority for the British and Hessians alike. Two small, but separate, bivouac areas were quickly laid out on the land side of the earthworks that faced the West Passage. Once completed, they fed and dismissed the troops to spend their first bivouac night on Conanicut Island.

My father, who had been farther back in the Hessian column, had his first chance to catch up with me.

"Well, son," he said, "You did real well today. That was quite a hike up and down the hilly terrain. The footing was pretty bad at times. But, you kept up with your own cadence. I made it a point to listen intently to see if you would goof up along the way. But you did all right. You can be proud of yourself. From what I understand, you will be staying close to Captain von Schwetzingen most of the time. He'll want you to be there if for some reason he has to give unexpected orders to the troops that may be scattered about the area from time to time."

"Papa, the terrain made it hard for me to carry the drum for such a long time. And it was real hot, to boot. And the dust, I heard some of the men coughing so hard, it got scary. I thought some of them would fall by the wayside. I know the distance from the ferry landing to the earthworks was not that great – we had marched greater distances in Portsmouth – but somehow today's heat and the pressure to get to the camp site quickly got to me and made things worse. I know I am going to sleep real well, tonight."

"Don't forget to brush the dust from your uniform. And, be prepared for a quick inspection in the morning. I imagine Captain von Schwetzingen will want to see clean uniforms. In the military, we don't care what went on the day before. Today is always a new day and you start out fresh, clean shaven and with clean uniforms. Remember that if you ever decide to make a career of this," my father cautioned.

The following morning, work parties were formed to accom-

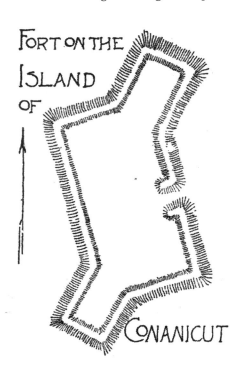

plish chores assigned for the day. Our Hessian contingent was detailed to perform manual labor enhancing the Fox Hill earthworks. As expected, I was directed to remain close to my company commander. The British, in turn, were given the responsibility of patrolling the shore and observing the bay for any movement coming from the mainland. A larger British contingent was dispatched to the Dumplins area, where they were to improve existing defensive positions that had been built earlier by an American militia unit that departed the island about the time the British convoy sailed into the West Passage.

My father was told the following week that the British had observed a group of soldiers on Dutch Island, in the West Passage of Narragansett Bay. The reporting patrol had been subsequently reinforced by the addition of 15 Hessian soldiers. When he mentioned this to me, I was excited.

"Do you think they will come over and attack us? Couldn't they be stopped before they landed if you see them coming? Maybe your captain should try to get some more soldiers from Newport," I said.

"Oh, don't get so excited," Papa replied, "They only observed a few of them along the shore on Dutch Island. I'd say they were scouts, watching us just as we are watching them. And, yes, if they were to come over and try to land, then, of course, we would do all we can to discourage them. And, if they were to come with a force larger than ours, I am sure our captain would call for assistance if needed. Don't forget, there are also quite a few Brits over near the Dumplings. They could be called to our side of the island if circumstances require. Knowing now that militia people may have set up camp on Dutch Island, there is no doubt in my mind that we will maintain a sizable unit of British or Hessians on Conanicut Island for quite a while."

"You know, Papa, it's real boring having to stay close to the captain all the time. I can't do anything. I just stand there, hoping he'll tell me to beat the drum with some signal he wants to get out to the others. But, that hasn't happened since we got here," I said.

"At least if we were in Newport, we would be marching around or practicing with other regimental drummers. Even so, I guess I'd have to go to school anyway. But while we are here, I don't have to. That's pretty good, too."

"Peter, I want you to understand that we are here to carry out whatever duties we are assigned. That's what soldiering is all about. I can't complain and neither should you. Don't you think I'd rather be in Newport, spending time with you and your mother instead of hiking to distant unknown places? Besides, you ought to get serious about school and the idea of wanting to learn. You did well not too long ago, but you seem to have forgotten that you are a brand-new drummer and not quite 11 years old. And by no means are you a soldier. But, regardless, you have responsibilities, just as I have responsibilities. I must provide for my family. I do so by serving my Prince at whatever places he sends me. Your responsibilities include going to school to learn all you can. One day, you too will have a family and the responsibility to provide for them. Do you understand?"

"Yes, I know, but it's just that I am so bored right now," I replied.

"Tell me, Peter, would you rather not be a drummer? If it's too boring, maybe you shouldn't be shouldering the responsibilities you accepted. We have to depend on our drum signals. Relaying and understanding them properly could mean life or death to many of us, including yourself," Papa reiterated.

"I'm fine, I'm fine. Yes, I do want to be a drummer, and a good one at that. I'm sorry if I got you upset. I didn't mean to."

"All right, Peter. I have to go now. It's time for me to see what my men have to say. Hopefully, they fully understand their duties and obligations. We sure are lucky the weather is holding up. It could all be a lot worse. We ought to be thankful for what we have. Have a good night, and cheer up. Tomorrow is another day."

The mission to Conanicut Island soon turned into a routine operation, with the troop assignments remaining much the same as originally designated, except that some of our Hessian soldiers were beginning to gather firewood and pile it up near the ferry landing on the east side of the island. That element of their work was hard, despite their use of the wagons and horse teams to move the heavy loads downhill to the storage site. Working in that vicinity allowed the soldiers to become acquainted with the two merchants that maintained small stores on the main travel route through the village.

One day, about the time our troops were preparing to return to Newport following their replacement by others, a local merchant complained to Captain von Schwetzingen that a tall Hessian had stolen several coins from his cash drawer. My father was assigned the task of finding the man and bringing him in for questioning. Since few Hessian soldiers were in a position to walk about the settlement freely, the alleged thief was quickly located. Common soldier Klaus Bechtel was identified by the merchant as the one who had stolen the money, upon which the captain ordered Bechtel held under guard, pending a hearing before a board of officers.

CHAPTER 16

In and about Newport

It was always a time of joy for my mother whenever her two soldier boys returned home from one of our field assignments. Forewarned of our arrival, she had done all the preliminary work to cook up a hearty meal of potato dumplings, served with a pork roast she barbecued in the open hearth.

"Hi," was my simple greeting when I walked through the door of our quarters on Thames Street.

"Hello, son, I am so happy to see you. You and your father always seem to be on the go. I miss the two of you very much while you are gone, and I worry and pray that you will be kept safe to return soon. How was your assignment on that island, what is it, Conanicut Island?"

"Oh, we had a fairly quiet time over there. But there was a lot of hard work for the soldiers, digging and improving some earthworks the rebels had built earlier. For me, it was uneventful. All I had to do was stick close to our captain and relay his messages to the troops with my drum from time to time. Then there was this one detail laying in hiding, watching a gang of colonists over on Dutch Island. There weren't many of them, but word was out to remain alert in case they try to come over and land on our side. They just stayed over on Dutch Island. Maybe they were watching to see what we were doing."

"Where's your father?" Mother asked.

"He's talking with the officers at the Colony House. Maybe they are planning our next assignment. Oh yes, before I forget, there was this one soldier who stole some coins from one of the merchants on Conanicut. They arrested him and he'll have to admit his wrongdoing before a panel of officers."

"Oh, that poor boy. Why did he do such a foolish thing? The coins won't do him any good, anyway. Now he'll probably be punished for acting like a silly little child."

"Well, he probably shouldn't have taken the money. Maybe he didn't think he'd get caught, or that someone might be watching him. That's what happened. The storekeeper said he saw him go into the drawer, and when he checked the contents later, he noticed that a few coins were missing. The only one who could have taken them was the fellow from our regiment," I said.

"The question is, Peter, did the merchant actually see him with coins in his hand?"

"I don't know any of that. I wasn't there. I didn't see anything. I'm just telling you of the talk that's been going around," I replied.

At about that time our sergeant walked in, and with outstretched arms headed for Mother. Hugging her, he said: "Oh, it's so good to be back. I never really enjoy being away. But, I am a soldier and we go where we are told to go, even though at times I'd rather stay at home with the two of you. This time there wasn't much going on, just some field work. Nevertheless, we always have to be on the lookout for things unusual, just to stay alive."

"Well," Mother said. "How about a roast pork dinner with potato dumplings, the way we had it back home on Sundays?"

"Well now, bring it on Madam. We soldiers could eat a horse right about now. I haven't eaten since daybreak and here we are at sunset. No wonder I am famished," Papa responded.

"Ha, right now I could put away twice as much as you, Papa," I mumbled. "I am starved."

"Listen boys, there is plenty for both of you and then some. So, go ahead and stuff yourselves. And later, go take your baths before you bed down for the night. I'll be sure to wake you at five in the morning so you won't miss your morning formation around the corner."

About two days later, I received word of my assignment as drummer when soldier Klaus Bechtel walks the gauntlet, his sentence for stealing from the merchant on Conanicut Island. Not having participated in this type of function before, I inquired about the procedures to be followed, the orders that would be given and the drum rolls I would provide during the soldier's walk. I was shocked to learn the gauntlet would consist of two lines of 100 soldiers facing each other, who would strike Bechtel's shirtless back with reeds when he is ordered to walk the gauntlet. To make things worse, Bechtel was sentenced to make the walk four times. While the punishment seemed excessive for the crime, Bechtel was being made an example as a warning to his comrades not to commit similar pranks.

As the sentence was being carried out, I beat the drum with all my might to drown out the sound of the reeds' whack, whack, whack, as they struck Bechtel's back. I was in agony myself, just having to participate in the ceremony. I couldn't recall anyone ever warning me that I might be required to perform this kind of unpleasant duty. By the time Bechtel started his third walk, he was badly bleeding from welts on his back. I felt very uneasy witnessing the cruelty of the sentence, which momentarily turned my

stomach. It was challenging to maintain my composure. But I quickly diverted my thoughts to thinking of better things, which allowed me to control my own plight until the sentence had been carried out. Upon dismissal, I ran to our home, telling myself I would never again complain of being kept idle or of being bored, or of being assigned to uneventful places or circumstances. Anything was better than witnessing such cruel punishment being administered.

The next time my father saw me, he asked: "Well, how did you do the other day when you beat the drum during the gauntlet affair? I can imagine observing the sentence being carried out may have been a bit disturbing to you. But you know, Peter, in the military, we must have discipline, and when there are infractions of acceptable behavior, corrective action must be taken or we'd open ourselves up to a free-for-all among the troops. That cannot be. We'd never be able to carry out our duties or fight as cohesive units. To do so, we must have discipline, including obedience of orders and adherence to the rules we accepted when we became soldiers. Don't worry, you'll be all right. Just do your job."

Still struggling with what I had experienced, I had little to say or add.

During the ensuing weeks, the British and Hessian regiments spent much of their time digging defensive positions on Rhode Island, also referred to as Aquidneck Island. The men were laying out defensive strong points, including earthworks, and digging trenches by hand in the anticipated path of any possible American advance from Portsmouth to the north.

Britain's Major General Pigot initiated these measures. He had assumed overall command within the Newport area following General Clinton's departure soon after our arrival. The presence of sizable numbers of militiamen and continentals along the shore of Tiverton prompted General Pigot to beef up his defenses of Newport as his top priority. Of course, I was there, beating my drum every morning when working parties assembled in town before marching to their assigned construction sites. If a detail's destination was in the nearby countryside, I sometimes requested permission to return to town so I could march again with some other unit. My superiors often provided favorable comments about me to my father, their Sergeant Bauer. They lauded my enthusiasm and eagerness to be of service. Even the British, who were organized into units separate from ours, made comments about me. They referred to me as the "one young Hessian boy who never failed to show up with his drum whenever a Hessian detail was about to take to the road." I became well known as one of the favored youngsters in the Ditfurth Regiment, particularly because of my love for my drum and the duties that went with it.

In marching about the parade ground in front of the Colony House and on my way back and forth on Thames Street, I noticed the same few people watching the soldiers drilling, and me beating the drum. I was beginning to recognize several of them from a distance, in particular, a well-dressed lady with white gloves, wearing a large and fancy bonnet. She was always there with her young dark-haired daughter by her side. She must be my age, I thought. Both apparently took a liking to me because their eyes followed me closely as I paraded around beating my drum. Knowing they were paying special attention to me made me extra conscious of my performance, so much so that I put on a bit of a display for them, for which I received their smiles in return. The little girl actually risked a subdued wave at me now and then, which made me feel even more appreciated and of importance.

On one of my occasional days off while walking around town, I encountered the lady and her daughter. As we neared each other, the lady asked, "Are you not the Hessian drummer boy whom we often see when we are in town?"

"Yes, Madam. I think so. I recognize you and your daughter. I have noticed you standing at the roadside watching the soldiers marching by," I replied.

"I should perhaps not say this, but you have impressed me as being a nice boy. You are always cheerful and seem to enjoy being a drummer, although many people in town despise the sound of your drum. It's so loud, and has a very deep and threatening sound."

"That's part of the fun for me. My drum makes the people take note that we are coming, and it gives them time to get off the street if they don't care to see us. But mainly, I enjoy marching ahead of the column, beating my drum. It helps the soldiers keep in step," I said.

"Yes, you do look smart. My daughter noticed that, too. I'd like to introduce her to you. I am Mrs. Humphrey and my daughter, Daphne, is with me. What is your name, young man?"

"Oh, I am Peter Bauer, I am a drummer boy of the Ditfurth Regiment. My father is a sergeant with the regiment, and my mother is here, too."

"Maybe you'd like to stop at our farm one day, when you have some free time. My husband grows wheat and rye, and also raises a few cattle. I imagine he could put you to work if you are available. He lost some of his help after our helpers left the island a year ago when the British fleet entered Narragansett Bay. We live nearby, just off East Road, about a mile from town," she explained.

"Oh, Mrs. Humphrey, my family has a farm, too," I said. It's in Hesse – that's where I come from. We lived there until my father's unit was called up to serve the King of England in his North American colonies," I continued.

"If you lived on a farm, then you must know something about farming," she replied.

"Oh, yes I do. I'm waiting to go back home to help Grandfather August and Uncle Franz with the farming chores."

"Well, Master Peter, you might want to ask for permission to work on a local farm. I am sure my husband would be pleased to provide you with food stuffs for any work you might do. We do know the troops do not have an overabundance of food, and that some soldiers are scrounging around where they shouldn't be. Anyway, think about it," Mrs. Humphrey concluded.

I smiled at her and her daughter, Daphne, who smiled in return and waved at me as they continued on their way.

Soon after, I told my parents about Mrs. Humphrey and what she had said.

After discussing the matter with Mother, my father had this to say:

"This is very interesting, since we have had several reports of a woman observing our activities around town. It may just be coincidence and perfectly innocent, but we have to remain alert. If we were back home, I wouldn't object to letting you work at a nearby farm, especially if there were a food shortage as we are experiencing. But somehow, I am concerned. First, there are attempts being made constantly to induce our personnel to desert to the other side in return for being given acres of land to settle here in America. And while we were still in the New York area, word was out that some of our men had been kidnapped from isolated posts and hustled away. These things make me wonder about this woman's motives."

"Oh, Papa," I responded, "She had her daughter with her, and she was nice, too. Both of them smiled at me. You don't see too much of that among the people here."

"Well, son, one might ask if bringing the daughter along wasn't a diversion of sorts. For the moment, I am against your visiting the Humphrey farm. Do you understand, Peter?"

"Yes, Papa," I replied with a voice reflecting my disappointment.

"I think I will suggest to my captain that one of our patrols check out the place on one of their routine sweeps through the countryside. Let's see what they come up with. Oh, on a more pleasant note, I want you to know, Peter, that our wagon master has finished rebuilding your drum. He showed it to me. It's just like new. The drum surfaces have been replaced and it has been re-strung. Besides giving it a fresh coat of paint, he replaced the rope and leather straps. Tomorrow, we can meet and then go pick up your drum. I suppose you'll say, 'It's about time,' but let me tell you, he did a great job and you ought to thank him when he gives the drum back to you. Bring the one you are now using with you. We'll have to return that one to the bandmaster."

"Gee," I replied. "Do you think the refurbished drum will be as good as the one I now have? Remember, it was water logged and broken when I found it."

"I am sure you can make some minor adjustments to get the sound you are looking for. After all, you are the star drummer in the regiment these days, so you ought to be able to handle the situation if there is a small problem, don't you think? I can tell you one thing: What you have is truly a trophy. No one can say they have a drum that floated down a river, got beat up badly and then was resurrected to serve another day. Think about it. Your drum is a one-of-a-kind instrument. Treat it properly and take care of it,"

Papa reminded.

When I saw the drum the next day, I was truly delighted and I let it be known. The wagon master was pleased to hear that I appreciated all the work and effort he had put into reconstituting the instrument for me. It didn't take too long for me to adjust to the drum, which alleviated my earlier concerns.

My father's inquiries into the strange woman's behavior did not turn up any derogatory information. She was identified as one of the guests the British had invited to the Christmas Ball that was held in the library hall soon after our arrival in Newport. Nevertheless, Papa preferred that I not wander about the country-side on my own despite the benefits that may be gained from occasionally working on the Humphrey farm. Mother agreed. As far as she was concerned, I was to stay in town unless assigned specific regimental duties. Our family discussed the matter and we all agreed, myself included, that I would not wander off on my own, despite my interest in seeing the pretty Humphrey girl, as I had implied repeatedly. Papa impressed on me that he could not afford to be distracted by my responsibilities as a drummer, and not to worry, since the girl wasn't going anywhere for now.

On British orders, the troops were detailed later in the fall to collect firewood for the garrison from all corners of Aquidneck Island. Although firewood had been collected earlier in the year, General Pigot accelerated the effort considerably. Under his latest orders, wooden fences, abandoned and dilapidated buildings, and even some wharves came under the ax. British and Hessian soldiers joined in carting the wood to pre-selected collection points close to Newport.

As usual, I was there beating my drum whenever soldiers were on the march. Whether they carried muskets, or axes, saws or pitchforks, made no difference. I just kept beating the drum, pro-viding the men with a steady marching pace, participating in the formations even when not ordered to do so. No one ever com-plained, least of all the officers and their noncoms. Their nor-mally loud shouting of cadence to keep the soldiers in step became unnecessary whenever the "boom, boom, boom" of my drum could be heard. And while the several regiments made good use of their own drummers, there were few that could match my enthusiasm and performance. Or so I'm told.

The winter of 1777-1778 was severe. Freezing temperatures and heavy snowstorms made life miserable, particularly for the unfortunate few who had been detailed to positions at remote locations along the shore facing Bristol and Tiverton. Those assigned to the British stronghold at Butts Hill were lucky to be housed in a wooden barracks constructed earlier in the year. They were saved the hardships of dealing with sub-zero temperatures and the snowdrifts that covered their open field dugouts in the immediate coastal areas from time to time. The loss of several lives due to the severity of the weather was a high price for the poor souls to pay who were deprived of adequate protection from the elements.

I was spared these trying field experiences, for I was detailed to remain in Newport with the bulk of the Ditfurth Regiment, where I was billeted in my family's quarters on Thames Street, not far from the Colony House and the garrison's drill field in front of that building. In effect, I had it pretty good. Early up in the morning, I would make my way to the Colony House, often through deep snow, where I would report to the headquarters detail and receive any orders they may have for me. Depending on troop assignments for the day, I could have a busy schedule waiting for me, or it could be a quiet time, a "dreary" day as I would call it.

On occasion of one of our routine family chitchats in early 1778, Papa shared some of his thoughts with Mother and me.

"For many months, we Hessians have been somewhat short-handed. You may not remember, but last May we lost two of our six regiments due to transfer and reassignment. This effectively decreased our strength from 3,000 to 2,000 men. That is quite a reduction of personnel. Luckily, the British garrison of 3,000 men has remained at full strength.

"As long as things are quiet and remain that way, we have little to worry about. However, over the past months, we have noticed increased activity among the colonists across the Sakonnet River in Tiverton. In particular, there seems to have been a gradual buildup of Continental troops, as well as among the militia elements on the other side. You know, when you concentrate so many men in an area, there must be a reason for it and a plan to use them. You don't just gather the troops, together so they can sit around doing nothing. These circumstances are of grave concern to us, and in particular, that we may have to face them with our reduced numbers.

The good news is that two new regiments will be joining us soon to make up for the troops that shipped out last May. I am telling you this so you don't worry in the event our opponents succeed in landing on the north end one of these days. If they want to try it, they will have to do it now, before our reinforcements arrive. I hear they are from Ansbach and Bayreuth, and they are seasoned in battle. They fought successfully against General George Washington in the New York area. These are the kind of fellows we'll need to fend off any massive assault by the American rebels."

"Papa," I asked. "Do you really think they will try something, knowing there are at least 5,000 or more British and Hessian soldiers just waiting for them to come?"

Mother chimed in, "If I were they and at odds with the King, as they say they are, I'd try anything to make the British leave. Half of the population seems to think that way."

"You are right, Anna," Papa acknowledged. "We expect they will make a move soon. Let them. We'll make their lives unpleasant and beat them back right into the Sakonnet River, whence they may come. And, if the Ansbach-Bayreuthers arrive before the Continentals come across with their supporting militia, we'd be able to stop them cold and turn them around before they are put ashore.

As far as the attitude of the population, that is a situation we did not expect to the extent you describe, Anna. But, I imagine the ones opposing us will have left by now, leaving the Tories behind who favor the British. Nevertheless, we all have to be alert and conscious of our surroundings. I'd be friendly, but careful. Especially you, Peter. Talk with the people, but be careful when they smile at you. They may be honest and mean well, but some might harbor ill thoughts about us Hessians and our British brothers in arms."

CHAPTER 17

The Battle of Rhode Island

Except for the continuing build-up of troops among Continental and militia elements in Tiverton, the summer of 1778 was quiet for the British and us Hessians, who were nonetheless kept on alert most of the time. Our morale was boosted considerably on July 16, when the two regiments from Ansbach and Bayreuth finally arrived and disembarked in Newport. Four days later, they were taken to Conanicut Island in flat boats, where they encamped at the Fox Hill earthworks and near the Dumplings on the ragged cliffs facing the open sea.

On July 29, word spread around Newport like wildfire that a French fleet had been spotted in the deep waters off Beavertail. This resulted in immediate withdrawal of the Ansbach-Bayreuth regiments from Conanicut Island. Anticipating a French attempt to enter Narragansett Bay to bottle up the British ships at anchor, several transports were scuttled in place in an effort to protect the inner harbor. Concurrently, all British and Hessian troops assigned to field locations as far north as Butts Hill were recalled to take up positions in previously prepared defensive works on the outskirts of Newport. It was a day of excitement and disorder because of all the ongoing action, the hustling about and the countermanding of orders sending the defending troops every which way. For me, it quickly became another first-time experience, another baptism by fire of sorts. Even I could tell there was panic among the soldiers in the streets of Newport. And certainly, there was no place for a drummer in this melee, with everyone hustling around, not knowing what was up.

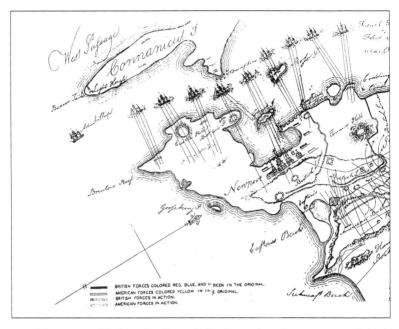

We were told that the French had cautiously sent one of their ships into the West Passage. While returning fire from the Battery at Fox Hill, their ship sailed further into bay, north of Conanicut Island. A similar exercise developed at the entrance of the East Passage. Eventually, the French fleet entered the bay in force, firing pointblank barrages of cannon balls at targets in the tightly populated areas of Newport. Panic was all around us as I ran for my life, finding temporary shelter in the cool cellar hole of one of the buildings, hoping to avoid the French cannon balls that were striking everywhere. Mother did likewise. She remained in the safety of a church, where she was attending the wounded soldiers brought in after the French bombardment. Even as their ships continued firing, British and Hessian details were in the fields near town, rounding up cattle from local farms and driving the animals to enclosures that had been set up earlier to receive them. Horses, pigs and sheep were also driven into the fortified Newport enclave in anticipation of a possible siege of the town.

I snooped around town when the bombardment let up to size up the horses that had been brought in. I thought I had found the right one for my father. The owner had told one of the soldiers driving the small herd that its name was Buckeroo. It was a wild fellow, kicking and bucking most of the time. I named it "Bock," German for a kicking goat. I was delighted knowing I would be able to give my father the good news that I had picked the right horse for him. But for the moment, there was no way of passing the word along. That would have to wait until later.

By nightfall, the French fleet was at anchor in Narragansett Bay, north of Conanicut Island, while our defenders were in their trenches and other defensive positions, sitting and waiting for what might come next. During the following days, Papa told us that a large contingent of French troops had landed on Conanicut Island and set up a hospital there.

Apparently hoping to link up with a French landing force of substantial size in Newport, the Continentals and their support troops crossed over from Tiverton on August 9, under the leadership of Major General John Sullivan, the American commander. Using forced march tactics, he was apparently determined to occupy as much of Portsmouth as possible to be ready for the big push on Newport in coordination with the French. He quickly encircled Newport from the land side and waited for some 4,000 French soldiers to join his 6,000 men for a joint thrust into the heart of our enclave centered in Newport.

Prolonged waiting for the French resulted in an extremely high level of anxiety among our defenders, as well as the attackers themselves. The tension topped out to Sullivan's dismay at the sighting on the horizon of an approaching British fleet. Without any further communication, the French admiral ordered his troops back to their ships, where they hauled anchors and set sails for the open sea and a hasty departure. Under no circumstances did the French want to be trapped inside the bay. Their objective suddenly was no longer to assist the Americans, but to engage the British fleet at sea, or so it seemed, according to my father's assessment.

They did, however, show their alliance to the Americans by delivering another devastating bombardment of Newport as they took to open waters. Their sudden departure left General Sullivan, who had moved most of his troops to the outer edges of Newport, in an extremely precarious position. He would have to face the defenders without the promised 4,000 Frenchmen, which called for a complete revision of his tactical plans. He opted to sit tight and wait for the French fleet to return, lest he be forced to loosen the noose on Newport and pull back to form a defensive line farther north, perhaps anchored on Butts Hill.

Nightfall prevented further operations of any significance on either side.

In the following days, the British kept close tabs on the movement of Sullivan's troops, while firing occasional salvos of cannon balls into their positions in the hope of keeping them unbalanced.

With the French fleet gone, I could again be myself. Though cheerful and forever ready to beat my drum, I remained conscious of the presence of Sullivan's soldiers on the high ground just east of the town. Still, I helped out wherever I could, even clearing heavy debris from inside the empty church buildings that were taken over as troop billets, a hospital and for the storage of emergency food supplies.

During the pre-dawn hours of August 28, a headquarters courier summoned my father to the Colony House, simultaneously alerting me to report to the parade ground within the hour.

On his arrival, my father met with the top non-commissioned officers of the several regiments billeted in town, and the officers of each of their units. Major John McBride, British adjutant to the local commander, greeted and addressed them.

"Our scouts have determined that the rebels have begun to retreat northward. The commanding general has ordered his Majesty's regiments to pursue the enemy along East Road, while General Lossberg's Hessians overtake and destroy the retreating forces on West Road. British and Hessian units in the field will operate independently of each other under the direction of their senior officer in charge, with overall command remaining with General Pigot, who is headquartered in Newport. Communications will be maintained by mounted messengers. All available units will jump off from designated assembly points near the juncture of East and West Roads at six a.m. That will be all. God be with you."

Even before the British adjutant had departed, Lieutenant Heinrich von der Hochburg joined the assembled senior Hessian officers who were gathered around General von Lossberg. He stood at attention, saluted and reported as follows:

"At the general's pleasure I have assembled a detail of 60 volunteers to serve as chasseurs in the absence of an assigned Jäger unit. My men are on standby and are prepared to move out at your command, your Excellency."

"Thank you, lieutenant. You and your chasseurs will be the first to head out on West Road. I am looking forward to some fast and decisive action as you proceed deeper into areas presently held by our opponents. You have great responsibilities. You are not only scouts, you have the traditions of our Jägers, our skilled hunters and woodsmen to uphold. From what I hear, you have assembled our most reliable men to serve with you. I wish you God speed, lieutenant."

"General, sir," he queried, "although our Jägers are usually not accompanied by drummers, I respectfully request we be allowed to proceed into enemy-held territory under the beat of one of our Hessian drums. I feel the rebels should hear us and anticipate their defeat as we approach."

"Request granted, lieutenant. Yes, Captain von Schwetzingen will assign one of his drummers to your chasseurs for the duration of the operation," he concluded.

The officers were then instructed to assemble their troops within an hour, ready to march. During this brief period, my father told me that I had been selected to accompany the chasseurs, which he considered a distinguished position. Much to his delight, he noticed that I was carrying my own drum. Placing his hand on my shoulder in a gesture of camaraderie, he said:

"Son, I am happy to see you will be carrying your own drum on this mission. I want you to know that I am really proud of you and always have been. Remember that. Everyone seems to like you. But, whatever you do from here on in, proceed with caution, and always be alert to your surroundings."

"Yes, Papa," I said. "I have some good news, a real surprise for you. In the corral in town, I came across a horse that would be perfect for you. It's a lively one. They just brought him in from one of the nearby farms, along with other horses and cattle, but this one needs some real breaking in. I figured you would be the one to do it, Papa. I know you were sorry having to leave Mamatschi with the Landgrave when you left the garrison back home. So, I asked the soldier in charge of the yard, to hang on to this one for you. It's called Buckey. I hope you don't mind what I have done. Maybe you can show me how to ride it when we get back."

"Peter, this makes me very happy. I am looking forward to getting back in a hurry so we can check Buckey out, together. That ought to be fun. But right now you should make every effort to meet up with Lieutenant von der Hochburg so he gets to know you. I also must hasten to get my troops lined up and ready for the march. God be with you, son. See you when we get back," Papa said as we headed our respective ways.

Lieutenant von der Hochburg was ready to head for the assembly area when I came strolling along with my big drum.

"Oh, there you are. I was wondering if they had really assigned a drummer boy to our chasseur detachment. Glad to have you with us, son."

I responded, "Sir, I am your tambour, Peter Bauer. I am good at drum signals. Right now, I'm ready to march whenever you say, sir,"

"All right, men, let's go. Drummer, fall in and give us our marching cadence!"

With that, the lieutenant called his men to attention, and I began beating the drum. The sudden rhythm of the beat must have stirred up the men who looked like they were coming to life again, as soldiers. I could tell their blood must have begun rushing through their veins as they quickly fell into a soldierly marching step.

This time, the "boom-boom-boom-boom-boom" cadence resounding from my drum was not at the slow Hessian pace. The lieutenant had told me to step up the cadence so his men could quickly adapt to moving along at a pace faster than normal. That was not only the lieutenant's wish, but an important feature of chasseur maneuverability, he said.

Ours was a colorful unit since it was made up of volunteers from the several regiments, each wearing uniforms with their own distinctive identification features. While all jackets were blue, the colors of the men's trousers varied. Some were white or striped, and while others were yellow, according to which regiment they belonged. By the time our detail arrived at our designated assembly point, three of Newport's six Hessian and Ansbach-Bayreuth regiments, with flags waving and drums beating, were approaching their given assembly points to receive further orders. Off to their right, I could see British Red Coat units forming into a column facing north on East Road, where they were allowed to fall out of their formation to relax and wait for new orders. As I looked about, I was impressed by the large gathering of troops. Though I had seen different uniform types around town on occasion, this was the first time I was able to observe entire groups of soldiers wearing identical uniforms and colors. To me, it all seemed like the troops were getting ready for a big parade, the major difference being there were hardly any onlookers. Most Newporters stayed in their houses, watching from doors and windows as the soldiers passed by. The local people were well aware of the recent French presence in the bay and on Conanicut Island, as well as of General Sullivan's siege of Newport, before his withdrawal in the direction of Butts Hill.

Before departing from the Colony House, our chasseuers were outfitted with shorter muskets so they could maneuver more freely. We proceeded northward at a hasty pace along West Road for a period, until one of the Lieutenant's men up front called out he had seen movement in a grove near a barn. At that moment, the men split up into four smaller groups, and after surrounding the area, surged forward into the direction of the reported enemy presence, shouting ear-piercing "Hurrahs." I picked up on the action by following the soldiers, beating my drum with vigor at double-time cadence.

I heard the musket fire as the chasseurs were rushing through the grove. At the far end, beyond the barn, a group of Continentals could be seen leaving the area in a northerly direction. Lieutenant von der Hochburg informed us that we had apparently run into General Sullivan's rear guard.

One of our chasseurs was killed by a musket ball as he stormed into the grove during the unit's northward advance. I saw several enemy wounded as I passed. Our chasseurs hurried along without stopping, trying to catch up with a group of militia men that were spotted falling back toward another section of high ground. As I

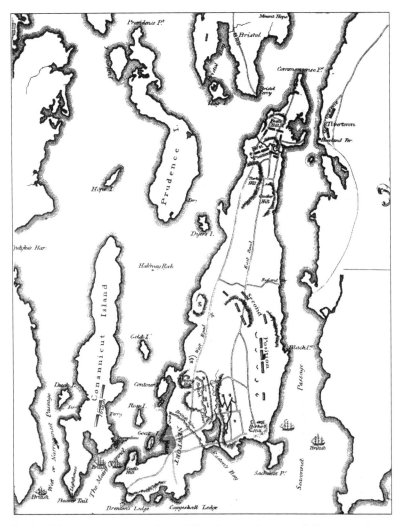

looked back, I saw the three Hessian regiments following along the road in an orderly fashion. I felt better knowing there were large numbers of friendly soldiers to our rear, and I kept up my accelerated drumbeat.

As tired as I was, I kept moving along like a good drummer boy. Several short slowdowns in our advance because of enemy fire allowed me to sit a moment here and there to catch my breath. However, as soon as the sound of musket fire subsided, I got back up on my feet and started all over, trying hard to keep up with the rushing soldiers, while dragging along my heavy drum. Eventually, Lieutenant von der Hochburg slowed down our forward charge to coordinate with the other regiments regarding the direction of our advance and any new objectives that might be assigned to us. He reported that it was agreed that the chasseurs would advance on both sides of the road, passing Turkey Hill, then cross a swampy area on the far side and attempt to storm a known enemy artillery position on the crest of Lehigh Hill. The three full regiments would in turn spread out over the fields to the west of the road and advance in a northerly direction on a broad front. Lieutenant von der Hochburg ordered a drum signal to ready the men and then jumped to his feet, shouting, "Vorwärts," forward. The chasseurs rapidly made their way past Turkey Hill and down into the marshy valley that came upon them as an unexpected surprise. I observed the men wading through murky water while jumping from one grass mound to another, until they reached solid ground on the other side. This was a challenge for me and my drum. My advance across the wet area was extremely difficult; I fell several times after stumbling over submerged tree stumps, and involuntarily wetted down my drum. I could tell the men were feeling miserable. Their woolen uniforms were of no help in the extreme heat of this late August day. I heard them cuss and mumble to themselves as they made their way forward.

To the rear, I heard the advancing regiments making their way across open fields, and then through the swampy area. I took a quick glance backward to reassure myself, and was delighted to see the breadth of the line of advancing Hessians following our chasseur unit. At that moment, General Sullivan's Militia opened fire from their positions on dry ground. They were joined by cannon fire from on top of the hill. As some of the chasseurs were falling, the lieutenant ordered a charge up the hill: "Vorwärts – marsch, marsch." The other Hessian units had closed their distance on our advancing chasseurs, giving the uphill battle greater momentum. We pushed forward, passing several fallen and wounded Continentals as the Jägers struggled in the extreme heat to get to the top of the hill.

Exhausted, some of the men began to fall back. It wasn't until the lieutenant reached a stone wall that he slowed down to catch his own breath and wait for me to catch up to him. Heavy musket

fire was coming from behind another stone wall, making it difficult for the chasseurs to stay close to him. When he saw they had
been pinned down by enemy fire, he said:

"Stay where you are, and stay low. I have to get the others out
of their predicament in a hurry. We'll be right back!"

"Yes, sir, I won't move. I'll stay here and wait," I responded
with a shaky voice.

Just as the lieutenant was making his way back toward the
men, the Americans launched a downhill attack to stop the
advancing Hessians from reaching the crest of the hill. During this
melee, several advancing militia men apparently noticed me sitting behind the stone wall with my drum. They were talking with
each other.

"Hey, look at that. A guy with a drum, right there," said one.
"Yeah, we ought to shoot 'im," another muttered.

"Why?" the first soldier asked. "He ain't going nowhere, and he
looks like a kid to me."

"Kid, my butt," the third man uttered. "If he had a gun, he'd kill
you."

"Yeah, but he ain't got no gun. He's got a drum, that's all," the
first soldier continued.

Then, a musket shot rang out, fired by a nearby militia man,
hitting my drum. The impact knocked the drum out of my hands
and as my body swung around, I bumped my head against the
stone wall, which knocked me out. I lay in a daze while the battle
raged on around me. I slipped under a bale of hay at the first
opportunity. The militia men who had been observing me earlier
were no longer there. They were likely well on their way down the
hill chasing some of our people back toward the swamp. I was
hearing gunfire at a greater distance now, and I crawled out from
under my pile of hay.

"Halt!" a voice shouted. "Halt, or I'll shoot!"

I was staring into the musket barrel of a black soldier. I didn't
know what to do, I was so scared. I just stood there without moving and could have cried.

"Come here, boy," the soldier said. "You are my prisoner, do
you understand? Don't try to run from me, 'cause I'll shoot you in

the eye, and your mama wouldn't like that. So, turn around and start walking up the hill to the road. Go on, move it."

I had learned a few words of English by now, but could certainly not understand a thing the black soldier was trying to tell me. I knew I was in a very precarious position. I was now in the hands of our enemies. They could do anything they wanted with me, I thought. And when I didn't understand the words "get a move on," the soldier jabbed his musket into my ribs. It hurt, and I knew then for sure what the soldier meant. When we reached the road, there were many more militia men and soldiers standing about, just talking and laughing. They had just repelled our uphill attack. While one of their leaders offered me a drink of water and a piece of dry bread, orders were being shouted among them that the Hessians were coming back. Without delay, the men quickly returned to their respective positions, leaving me and my escort standing at the side of the road.

A young officer yelled at the black soldier: "Escort him to Butts Hill and turn him over to the officer in charge."

"Yes, sir," he responded, pointing me in the direction to go.

To our rear, in the distance, the battle was on again. Our Hessians had retreated all the way to Turkey Hill and after regrouping, had returned to the earlier battle site with the same objective of silencing the enemy cannons on the hill.

I had a smile on my face when the soldier turned me over to one of the Continental officers at Butts Hill. I had been here before. My father and I had helped build several storage huts here not too long ago. The officer was a serious man. He quickly ordered me to be locked up in one of the smaller sheds, advising one of his men to make sure the door hasp was secure. I was then left by myself for the night. As I watched through the cracks in the door and walls, Butts Hill seemed overcrowded with men and material. However, everyone appeared busy packing and loading wagons with equipment. I didn't quite understand what they were up to. Were they preparing to head north and leave Rhode Island, or were they getting ready to march on Newport once more? The night was cold in the shed and I had plenty of time to think about the day's happenings, but I had no idea how the events I witnessed actually ended. I could only recall seeing myself behind enemy lines as a prisoner and learning that the Hessians were counter-attacking after having been repelled earlier. I prayed for my father, whom I had not seen since the early hours of the day, hoping he made it safely through the battle in the fields near the swamp. I knew my mother must be safe in Newport, knowing the enemy was not that close to town anymore. Somehow, I fell asleep as I watched the campfires burn down. When I woke up during the night to relieve myself, I noticed that much of the activity within the Butts Hill earthworks had calmed down, with most of the occupants sound asleep, except for the loading operations that continued at the far end of the fort. I noticed the area near my cage was dimly lighted by a partially burned-out fire. I thought that now was the time to escape.

I stretched hard to get a better look at the door latch, noticing it was secured with a stick that had been dropped into the eye of the assembly. Knowing this, I began scrounging around the floor in the dark until I found a long thin piece of wood I was able to slip through the slats in the door sufficiently to loosen and remove the peg from the latch. I succeeded after several desperate tries and then slipped out of the door into the open, where I first hid in some brush behind the shed. Soon after, I moved further away to hide among some felled trees that had been placed as obstructions along the perimeter of the earthworks by the British when they held the site.

Just before sunrise, General Sullivan's Butts Hill contingent got off to an early start, moving their wagons and cannons out of the defense complex and onward in the direction of the dock facing Tiverton and Fort Barton on the other side. When a guard came to get me, I was no longer in the shed, where I had been kept for the night. He made a haphazard search of the immediate vicinity and failed to find me in his apparent haste. Soon after, the militia and Continentals left the hill without further delays.

I did not move from my hiding place for quite a while. I wanted to be sure that everyone had left before I crawled out. When I did, I looked around to be sure no one else was there. The only thought in my mind was to head south to re-join my unit if they hadn't returned to Newport. Just as I was about to leave the earthworks, I saw a scouting party wearing red coats coming up the hill to where I was. I became all excited. They were British.

I waved my hat, yelling: "Hallo, me friend, me Hessian."

Four British scouts came toward me, each with a big smile on his face.

"Well now, what would a young lad like you be doing out here all alone so early in the morning," their leader asked?

"Well, jock," one of his comrades said laughingly, "he must be the Hessian boy who captured the fort single-handedly, ha ha."

The others joined him in a hearty laugh.

Still, the leader asked:

"What were you doing here?"

"I was prisoner. Me drummer boy for Lieutenant von der Hochburg yesterday. Black soldier take me here. Now you come."

"So, you are the Hessian drummer boy everyone has been talking about? Guess you must have been doing a good job. But, where is your drum?" the leader continued.

"Musket ball make bad hole in drum. Drum 'kaputt ,'" I replied sadly.

"All right, son, I am ordering you to head south on West Road until you find your unit or get back to Newport, where you should report to the Colony House. Cheerio, young fellow. Hope you find a new drum. Keep your eyes open, there may just be one along the road somewhere."

The soldiers laughed again as I started my long and lonely hike toward Newport.

CHAPTER 18

Setbacks

It was not an exciting walk for me, at least not as far as my sore feet were concerned. I blamed my condition on the swamp where I first got my feet wet. In all the excitement that followed, I had not found time to take off my wet socks and shoes, at least not until I bedded down in the shed for my night in captivity. Although taking my shoes and socks off during the night was perhaps the best thing I could think of, I had been hesitant about it, not knowing what plans my captors had for me. So I limited the time laying there without shoes and socks. Their dampness contributed to my resultant discomfort and pains. I had such a long hike ahead of me and no drum to speed up my own pace. In a way, I was glad. My feet were too sore to walk fast, and I was beginning to limp. So I just moped along, my mind in another world, trying to make the hurt go away.

After cutting across a field in the direction of West Road, I ran into three soldiers whose uniforms were not quite familiar to me. But hearing them speak in my own language as I approached was of some relief. One can never know who might be wandering about in the countryside after a battle and the withdrawal of troops from both sides. I kept telling myself: Best be real careful.

Standing in the middle of the road, the first soldier ordered me to stop with a hard, "Halt!"

Oh, I stopped all right. Who were they, anyway?

"What are you doing out here?" the second soldier asked.

"I am the drummer of the Ditfurth Regiment. I was captured

by the rebels yesterday when they counter-attacked. They all left the Butts Hill fort early this morning. I hid in the underbrush and they didn't see me when it was time for them to leave. A British patrol up the road told me to head back to Newport."

"If you are a drummer, where is your drum?"

"A musket ball went right through it and wrecked it. It was no good after that. Besides, I was taken prisoner about then and couldn't take it with me anyway," I replied, and then asked: "What regiment are you from?"

"We are from the Bayreuth regiment. We and the fellows from the Ansbach regiment were sent out here to relieve you Hessians."

Some of them are still over there in the field, picking up debris and burying the dead from yesterday's engagement," the soldier answered.

"Were there many dead?" I inquired.

"I'm not sure, but it looks like they had to dig a pretty big grave to bury them all. I'd say, from what I've seen, there must have been at least 30 dead altogether.

"There were quite a few wounded, too, on our side. Then, there are some rebels across the creek that have to be buried as well," the soldier replied.

"It is all so sad to think about and see," I uttered in a broken voice.

"Well, be thankful that you are still walking around. You know, when you charge an enemy you never know how far you will get. I always give thanks when it's over," he said.

The first soldier then suggested I be on my way because of the long hike ahead of me to reach Newport. He offered me a piece of bread and cool drink of water before I continued my trek southward.

After several hours of limping along the road and many stops to rest my feet, I finally entered Newport, where I headed straight for our family's quarters on Thames Street. When I walked through the door, I was surprised to see the field parson, Johann Hofmeister, sitting next to Mother, holding her hands. She was crying.

"Mother, what's the matter? Why are you crying?" I asked.

"Oh, Peter. Where have you been? When the regiment returned this morning and you were not with them, I could have lost my mind. Where were you?"

"Mother, I am here. I am fine. There is no need to cry," I replied.

At that point, Parson Hofmeister said:

"Son, your mother just learned that your father, Sergeant Bauer, was killed in yesterday's skirmish with the American Continentals off West Road. I know this is hard for you, as it is for your dear mother, but you need to be strong at times like this. Remember, he loved you both, that's why he brought you along. Now we can only pray and give thanks for the time you were allowed to spend with him. I know he was a good father to you, Peter. He would have given the world to see you grow into a kind and considerate man, the type of person he himself was. Your role in life must now change from being a boy to assuming some of the responsibilities your father can no longer discharge. Your mother will now need you more than ever before. Overnight, you have become a pillar of strength for your mother. She will be depending on you, Peter, despite your very young age. She will need your help, remember that."

I listened intently, holding my tears back until the sorrow of losing my father, my papa, took over. With my arms around my mother's neck, I sobbed, almost out of control. Sorrow and disappointment at plans gone awry made me ask time and again:

"Why, why, why my father? What did he do wrong? He was always so good to me. Everyone liked him. I wanted him to have Buckey when he got back to town." I sobbed.

"Who is Buckey?" Mother asked.

"Oh, that's that real lively horse they brought in a few days ago. He would have been so perfect for my papa. He liked horses. Remember when he came home riding the Landgrave's horse, Mamatschi? I could tell how much he loved that horse. I just wanted to make him happy and show him how much I loved him. Now, I can't," I whimpered.

"Peter," the Parson interjected. "Your father knows of your love, and for this, he will see to it that you are blessed in your own life's undertakings. Have faith, son, and all will be well. Hold his image before you at all times and smile when you feel he is near you, for he will be."

"Whose horse was it, Peter?" Mother asked.

"I think it may have belonged to the Humphreys, you know the farmer whose wife and daughter I told you about?" I responded.

"Oh, yes. Now I understand. Too bad you can't give them their horse back, but maybe you can let them know what a beautiful horse it is and that you had wanted your own father to ride it."

"Mother, are you telling me I can go to the Humphrey farm to tell them?"

"Let's see how things are, now that the American Continentals have left Rhode Island and the French fleet is gone. If it's safe enough for you to visit the farm, maybe you could go. Just a friendly visit, you understand?"

After the discussions had drifted to more common matters, the parson hugged us both and left, telling us he had a few more stops to make to report on the condition of several wounded soldiers who were at the hospital. Mama assured him that she would return to work at the medical facility the following day.

After a hot bath, a hearty meal and a good night's sleep, I reported to unit headquarters at the Colony House. I had been listed as missing by the chasseurs after they withdrew under heavy fire from a unit of black soldiers. My father's company commander, Captain von Schwetzingen, was happy to see me alive. He offered words of encouragement on the untimely death of my father, his own Sergeant Bauer, as he referred to him, explaining that I could continue to serve as drummer for the regiment, and also that arrangements would be made for me to receive a new drum. I felt good and reassured. I forgot all about my sore feet.

On one of my days off sometime in October, Mother allowed me to venture out of the town limits of Newport to visit the Humphrey farm located a mile off East Road. I was lucky; Mrs. Humphrey was there and her daughter, Daphne, was busy hanging clothes on the line.

"Oh, how nice of you to visit us," Mrs. Humphrey said when she saw me.

"Well, Madam, I wanted to stop over before, but circumstances on the island were such that I was prevented from coming."

"We had quite a few Americans from militia units out here a while back and were not sure if we would ever see you again. But they pulled back and now, as I understand, they are on the other side of the Sakonnet in Tiverton again. I don't imagine they will come again, unless the French are serious about assisting them."

When Daphne had finished pinning up the clothes, she joined us, saying: "Hello, Peter. I am happy to see you and see that you are all right after all the shooting that was going on around here a few weeks ago."

"I am happy to be here, Miss Daphne," I replied.

I was then introduced to Mr. Humphrey, who came into the house for a cup of coffee.

"How are you, young man. I understand you are a real pro with your drum."

"Oh, I love my drum, sir. But, I have to wait for a new one. The one I had before got shot up, all splintered and damaged beyond repair," I replied.

"Well, I am sure you will do all right," the farmer noted. "By the way, I understand you worked on your family's farm before you came over here. If you are still here next year, you know, I could probably use an extra hand every now and then. So, keep in touch and let me know. You'll be 12 or 13 by then, right?"

"I'll be 12, next year, sir," I said.

"That would be fine. And you'd be a bit stronger, too."

"Oh, Mr. Humphrey, I wanted you to know that the horse that was confiscated from you a few weeks ago was such a beautiful animal, I tried having it set aside for my own father to ride. It seemed so special. But, he was killed during the recent battle out along West Road. I had told him of the horse and he was anxious to ride it. In fact, he was going to teach me to ride. Now, that won't be possible. But I did want you to know that your horse is special. I was told to call him Buckey, is that right?"

"Yes, young Buckey was my own favorite, but the British took him. I only hope he is being treated well and that I might get him back one day," he replied. Soon after, he extended condolences on behalf of his family on the loss of my father, which I thought was very kind of him.

After visiting for an hour or so, I bid the Humphreys goodbye. I was again asked to be sure to come back, and if for some reason that did not materialize, should I be shipped home instead, then I should give some thought to coming back one day.

As this was said, Daphne's eyes lit up and she commented: "Oh yes, Peter, if you ever decide to come back to America, please be sure to stop in to see us. I would like that very much."

I turned toward her with a shy smile on my face, saying: "Miss Daphne, if I work hard enough, maybe I could come back one day."

The winter of 1778-1779 turned out to be another time of great difficulty for us all in Newport. Although British ships were re-supplying our garrison, the frequency of their visits to Narragansett Bay was less than was hoped for at this outpost. Trips to the areas of Long Island Sound and nearby islands to collect firewood became routine, else there would be no home fires burning in the Newport enclave in the height of the winter. Extremely low temperatures and excessive accumulations of snow made life in town unbearable at times. We heard that some soldiers froze and died at some of the remote outposts on the island, and food became a rare commodity.

Newport was held by the British until mid-October 1779, when we all embarked on a fleet of ships destined for new areas of assignment farther south along the east coast. During the past year in Newport, things had been quiet and life had settled into a boring routine of little to do. I marched about with a new drum when called to do so, but there were few challenging moments in the lives of the soldiers, except for building additional fortifications around Newport and across the bay on Conanicut Island.

We learned that some of the troops that moved from Newport were put ashore in New York, with others continuing on to destinations further south, where they linked up with contingents already there. During the next two years, battles were fought in many places, the most significant at Yorktown, Pennsylvania, where the French fleet applied pressure on the British and Hessians from the sea, while American troops on foot supported by several thousand French soldiers succeeded in forcing the surrender of Britain's General Cornwallis and his troops in October 1781.

Soon after the surrender, some of the troops were returned to Europe, women and children included. I had been transferred to Charleston with elements of the von Ditfurth Regiment, along with units of the von Huyn Regiment, in due course.

It was not until mid-July 1783 that I was able to embark at Sandy Hook for my return trip home. I had been nine years old when we left and would be 17 going on 18 by the time I reached Kirchdorf, my home town.

The voyage back to Europe was an experience I had hoped to avoid. However, there was no other way to cross over than by way of the vast Atlantic Ocean, with its rough seas, stormy weather and many unpredictable dangers that could pop up out of nowhere. My present experiences closely approximated those of our earlier crossing. Bad food and seasickness were once again the norm, and I wished I had stayed behind in America rather than becoming a hero by challenging the sea.

Despite my misgivings, I managed pretty well, telling myself I had become a man in my own right, withstanding nature and whatever it had thrown my way. My journey finally ended in Bremerlehe on October 8, the place whence we had departed over eight years before. Things had been different at that time. My father had been with us, and my mother was busy sewing up a uniform for me. Now I was

LCS

coming home alone, older and maybe a bit wiser, but still alone. My father was no more and my mother had returned to Hesse long before me. I was now taller and wearing a uniform supplied by the regiment, since I had outgrown the outfit Mother had made.

Moving the homecoming troops from Bremerlehe to their garrison towns required another month of strenuous duty, hiking up and down hills and valleys, through villages and past churches and monasteries, with rest stops in between. This time around, sore feet and blisters were a common occurrence for many of us.

"That, too, will pass," I thought. "Soon it will be over and I will be back home. I want to be there to be of help to mother."

As the overland convoy passed through Hessian territory, some of the men were getting restless, particularly as we were approaching their own garrison towns. Once there, the local unit would be dismissed promptly to allow the soldiers to return to their homes and families without any undue delays. Everyone was given a 10-day furlough after which they were to return to their respective units for further duty as appropriate.

The Marburg group, to which I belonged, was the last to be dismissed. I had actually had the longest hike. As I looked down the hill from the castle and into the valley below, I remembered well the day I visited my father and the opportunity I was given to march around the drill area with the Landgrave's soldiers. That was so exciting at the time, so much fun. And later, when our long wagon train headed out and through town with all the people watching and cheering was something I would never forget. My homecoming was nothing like it. It was rather somber, with little excitement and no one cheering the soldiers on. It was as though no one knew we were back. Maybe they didn't care. We had not won the war for the King, but we sure had fought successfully and with honor.

Thinking about these things, I continued the last leg of my trip on a sour note. I was wrapped in deep thoughts, hiking all the way to Kirchdorf. While away, I had learned to march long distances, simultaneously strengthening my leg muscles so they would carry the weight of my body for miles on end without giving out. I was humming an old Ansbach marching song I learned in Newport, just to keep up my spirits and marching cadence. It was almost as though I was moving along as an army of one, satisfied at maintaining a smart marching rhythm. Doing so reminded me of the

way my father strutted along when he came home on furlough some years ago. I smiled then, and now I smiled at my own marching habits.

I laughed quietly as I approached the gate to the farm from the road. I opened the heavy squeaky gate and quickly scanned the interior of the farmyard like an eagle, with eyes that wouldn't miss a thing, something I had also learned in the King's colonies. Everything looked well as I headed for the door to the living quarters and knocked.

Mother opened the door and yelled with joy:

"Peter is here, Peter is back. Come everybody, see Peter."

I reached out and put my arms around her neck, giving her a big hug, saying:

"It's been so long, Mother. How have you been? I hope all is well with you. I missed you so much. Nothing went right for us after we left Newport. We were transferred several times after that. And when you left, what a mess it was. But I'm glad I am home again and can take care of you, just like Papa would have wanted me to."

Uncle Franz came to the door to welcome me. He was carrying a baby in his arms. Smiling, he said:

"Come Peter, say 'hello' to your cousin, Gerhard."

I was very surprised to see my uncle with the baby. He wasn't married when we left years ago and said then that he wouldn't have any children. So, what was this all about?

"Uncle Franz, I didn't know you got married. Mother never had a letter from you in all the years we were away, except when you notified us that Grandfather August had died," I said.

"Anna," Uncle Franz asked, "didn't you let Peter know that we married soon after you returned from overseas?"

"No, I'm sorry to both of you. It was difficult for me to write, even though I am very happy being married again and having a baby son. I didn't know where you were, Peter. I never knew what happened to you. I was in sorrow and withdrawn for a long time, not knowing if you had survived the war in the British colonies.

"So, what is Gerhard, is he my brother or my cousin?" I asked.

Uncle Franz replied: "He is both. He's your Mother's son, a

half-brother to you, and he is my son, and your cousin. Don't let anything like that bother you. You are my nephew and you will always have a job here and a place to live. Little Gerhard still has a few years to go before he will be ready to inherit the farm."

I swallowed hard. Uncle Franz had said that Gerhard would someday inherit the farm. That's right. Gerhard is the son of the oldest of the Bauer brothers and therefore the rightful heir to the farm.

"Come in, Peter, sit down. Have something to eat. Oh, I am relieved and so happy you are back. I always worried when you were not around. How long can you stay with us, Peter? Are you going to be mustered out soon?" Mother asked.

"Well, Mother, I should be mustered out in a few months, when I am 18. I will be stationed in Marburg until then. At least I'll be close to home," I replied.

"Maybe you can help out on the farm until you are discharged," Uncle Franz suggested.

"Oh sure. If I can get away, I'll be happy to do that," I said.

JHS

"And, as I said," Uncle Franz continued, " you can have a regular job here after that."

"Thank you, Uncle Franz. But I do want to find out what's going on generally before I make up my mind to settle down. I have been on the go for almost eight years. I've got to think out what it means to settle down. I have seen our village, but I have also seen other parts of the world. There is a lot to it. Different places, different people. Right now, I am confused. I need to think it out. I have a furlough. If it's all right with you, I'll stay here, help out as much as I can, and in a week or so, I'll go back to Marburg and my unit and give it all some more thought.

Is that all right with you, Uncle Franz?"

"Sure, Peter," he responded.

CHAPTER 19

A New Beginning

After my 10-day furlough, I reported to the regiment in Marburg for further duty until my discharge later in 1784. I had given much thought to the options open to me, and while I wanted to stay close to Mother to be of help to her when needed, I felt the thought of eventually inheriting the farm would no longer be a possibility, now that a male-child had been born to Uncle Franz, the rightful owner of the family farm.

Though withholding a decision on my future plans, I next approached Parson Johann Hofmeister to ask if he would draft an enlistment request to the Landgrave for me. Following is the letter he wrote on my behalf:

> *To His Excellency*
> *The Landgrave Friedrich of Hesse-Kassel*
> *Having faithfully served your Excellency in the Ditfurth Regiment as a drummer boy in North America from 1776 - 1783, I wish to respectfully request your Excellencies' favor of enlisting me as a full time member of the Regiment following my discharge during the early months of 1784.*
> *I wish to continue serving your Excellency in honor and memory of my father, Sergeant Karl Bauer who gave his life in the face of the enemy during the Battle of Rhode Island on August 28, 1778.*
> *This humble request submitted by:*
> *Peter Bauer, Drummer, Ditfurth Regiment*
> *January 10, 1784*

To my greatest surprise, the Landgrave responded favorably and expeditiously, much faster than I had expected.:

Prince Friedrich II
Landgrave of Hesse-Kassel

Having favourably considered your request for enlistment in the Difurth Regiment, you, drummer Peter Bauer, of Kirchdorf on the Lahn, are hereby notified that you are accepted for enlistment in the Difurth Regiment for a period of ten years. You will be designated as Regimental Tambour with service to commence on or about the 30th day of March in the year of our lord one thousand seben hundred and eighty four.

By authority of the Landgrave,

General Von Ditfurth of Marburg

Realizing the Landgrave had accepted my request for enlistment and invited me to serve Hesse in the Regiment of my own choice, I felt to decline would be like turning my back on the Prince, my Father and my deep inner feelings for him. Here I was faced with making a very serious and far-reaching decision that could shape my life from this time forward. I love the farm and my family. I was hoping to inherit the farm one day, but I also have a special attachment to the military, the environment where my father served and where I learned my first marching steps.

I find myself at a crossroads, and despite the several options open to me, I feel compelled to accept the Landgrave's offer. I will enlist as the regimental tambour of the Ditfurth Regiment .

Only time will tell if I made the right choice.

About the Author

Walter Schroder was born in Rhode Island, the son of German immigrants. He spent the years of his youth in Germany, where he attended school and was drafted at age 15 to serve with an anti-aircraft battery during WWII. Based on his American birth, he was permitted to join the U.S. Army at Marburg, Germany in 1948.

Discharged in America, he completed a 31-year civilian career with the Defense Department and subsequently served as training officer for the Rhode Island Emergency Management Agency for four years.

His special interests in military history resulted in the publication of five popular non-fiction titles, including his autobiography, "Stars and Swastikas: The Boy Who Wore Two Uniforms." He has lectured extensively and appeared on NBC10 Timelines and public television. In 2007, he was inducted into the Rhode Island Heritage Hall of Fame.

Public acceptance of his 2005 narrative: "The Hessian Occupation of Newport and Rhode Island, 1776-1779," prompted him to expand on the factual material by adding fictional characters. "The Hessian Drummer Boy of Newport" serves as a history lesson for young people in a readable and understandable format.

7367036R0

Made in the USA
Charleston, SC
23 February 2011